MORE CLUES TO THE EXCITEMENT ABOUT ROBERT BARNARD

CORPSE
IN A
GILDED CAGE

ROBERT BARNARD

A DELL BOOK

Published by
Dell Publishing Co., Inc.
1 Dag Hammarskjold Plaza
New York, New York 10017

Dell ® TM 681510, Dell Publishing Co., Inc.

ISBN: 0-440-11465-9

Reprinted by arrangement with Charles Scribner's Sons
Printed in the United States of America
October 1985

10 9 8 7 6 5 4 3 2

CORPSE
IN A
GILDED CAGE

CONTENTS

CORPSE
IN A
GILDED CAGE

CHAPTER 1

CHETTON HALL

Chetton Hall, that splendid monument of Jacobean domestic architecture, lay basking in the early evening sun. The coolest place was under the elms of the Countess's Mile, where the wife of the fourth Earl had dallied on horseback with her groom, Richard Mont. Tiny breezes from the river drifted over Long Meadow, where the famous herd of Herefords, established by the sixth Earl, 'Farmer Jack', warmed their velvety hides and moaned contentedly. The lovers from Chetton Lacey who lay on the haystack in Parson's Field felt the last ripples of the breeze on their burning flesh, and they too moaned in pleasure. But the breeze petered out long before it could reach the environs of the great house. Not a breath fanned the Dutch Garden, which looked frizzled and ill-cared-for. The great stone balustrade overlooking the fountain might, it seemed, have burned at a touch, and the steps leading down from it sent up a distorting curtain of heat haze. Only the fountain, where Charles James Fox had bathed when drunk, seemed to be actively enjoying the June warmth, dancing hectically in the sun's rays and scattering an ecstasy of shimmering light.

But the most splendid triumph of the sun was on the house itself. To turn from the fountain to the West Front was to be confronted with liquid gold. All the windows swam in light, and swayed like waters in a bay, flowing round the baroque splendours of the Queen's Entrance, through which Anne of Denmark passed on her progress to the West Country. Behind the Front, cooler as was fitting, lay the massive Blenheim Wing, added by the first

Earl in the years after that battle, in which he had fought. But it was the glorious central block, begun in 1610 by Sir Philip Spender, the King's Secretary of Monopolies, that greeted the sun as an equal, confident in its beauty as any king's favourite, monumentally self-possessed, arrogant in the knowledge of what it had been, what it was, and what it always would be.

In the Green Drawing-Room the twelfth Earl of Ellesmere addressed his Countess.

'Would you like another cup of tea, Elsie? I think I can squeeze one from the pot.'

The Countess considered, her mouth set in a determined droop of discontent.

'No-ow. It'll only be stone cold. Practically cold anyway, once you've trailed it through all them bleeding corridors.'

The Earl, a man of congenital good-nature and optimism, chuckled.

'You're not far out. I don't know how they stood it here: nothing but half-cold tea and half-cold dinners. It's not what I'd call a life of privilege.'

'If that's privilege, give me Clapham any day,' agreed the Countess.

'Makes you think how lucky we've been, eh, Elsie?' said the Earl, settling his comfortable girth back in the green and gilt sofa and gazing around him with a good-humoured expression. 'Our own home, nearly paid for, everything just as we like it, neat and ship-shape and cosy as a Christmas card . . . I don't think this place could ever be cosy, do you, Elsie?'

'Cosy?' said the Countess, gazing disparagingly round the long and elegant drawing-room, designed and furnished for the third Earl by James Wyatt (who had seduced his Countess the while). She eyed gloomily the straight-backed green silk sofas and chairs, the stucco reliefs, the ormolu clock, the classic mantel. She shook her head gloomily.

'Never in a million years. I can't think why they put up with it, your lot. Can't have been much like you, Perce. You always did hate a draught. But they existed in this draughty old barn, year in, year out. Nasty great hole. Cold as sin, even with the sun blazing away outside like now. Miles to walk, even if you only want to spend a penny. Nearest neighbour three miles or more away. Brrr. Gives me the shivers just to think of living here much longer.'

The Earl nodded, and drained his cup.

'Right you are, as usual, Elsie. If I want to walk miles I'd rather do it on Clapham Common.'

He placed his hand over the olive-green cardigan that covered his substantial tummy and gazed around him with unabated good humour. His face took on that reflective expression well-known to regular customers at the Clapham iron-monger's where he had worked prior to being summoned to his high destiny—for he was a man whose homely philosophizing was appreciated in his own circle, where they had an old-fashioned liking for someone who could voice what oft was thought but ne'er so well expressed.

'From now on, Elsie, this is going to make us count our blessings. Look on the bright side. Not take things for granted. We're going to appreciate having had to go through all this when we get home.'

'*When* we get home,' repeated the Countess, whose expression had taken on new shades of lugubrious foreboding. She was well known in Haig Street, Clapham, as the Cassandra of the locality, with a relish for dissecting present discontents and a gift for the accurate prediction of woes to come. Few went to the bad in Haig Street, Clapham, without their downward path having been mapped out in advance by Elsie Spender. 'When's the operative word. It's been — what? — six weeks already, and they've been the longest six weeks of my life. I want to see an end to it, Perce.'

'I'll talk to old Lillywaite tomorrow,' said the Earl. 'Give him an ultimatum.'

'Hmmm. You'll be lucky if you get a straight answer out of him. You know lawyers. I'm telling you, Perce, I'm not spending a winter in this great barn, not for all the tea in China. I'd have gone home long ago except it'd have meant leaving you here on your own. Two peas rattling around is bad enough, but one would have been ridiculous. You'd have gone off your rocker.'

The Earl looked at her with genuine, ripe affection.

'That's my Elsie. Best wife a man ever had. Anyway, you can't go now. Not with the kids and the grandchildren coming. It's going to be the birthday party of a lifetime, and I'm going to enjoy every minute of it. It'll be a joy just to see their faces when they clap eyes on this place. Their eyes will pop — eh, Elsie?'

Chuckling again, the Earl of Ellesmere ambled over to the tall windows that dominated the west wall of the drawing-room.

'Not to mention when they see the grounds,' he added. 'Some garden, eh?'

He gazed with some complacency over his domain, over the formal gardens, the balustrade and steps leading down to the fountain, over the elegant avenue of trees and on to the meadows and fields beyond, stretching almost to the horizon. Perhaps he felt, in the pit of his stomach, some slight twinge that told him that to be master of Chetton was something.

'One thing about this place,' he said at last. 'The kiddies will have plenty of room to play about.'

The Countess had shifted her motherly bulk from her chair, and now came over to join him companionably by the window. But she was not a woman who allowed her disposition to be lightened by her husband's sunnier one. She viewed the rolling prospect without favour.

'Countryside!' she said, witheringly. 'I've always hated the countryside. I haven't said so because it doesn't do, but I have. I've always hated picnics: nothing but wasps and ants and creepy-crawlies. Of course the Common is different, because there's always people around. Country is miles and miles of nothing, with cows on it. I hate cows. And I'm not having the kiddies playing with them cows over there.'

'Trust Dixie for that,' said the Earl. 'She'll see they don't go anywhere near.'

At the mention of her daughter-in-law the Countess's lugubrious countenance became twisted into a *moue* of distaste.

'Hmmm,' she said, gazing ahead with vatic foreboding. 'I don't think you're going to impress Dixie with this place, Perce. It's not her style at all. Remember her in the Brighton Pavilion?'

The Earl gave a reminiscent laugh.

'Don't I ever! Came on a bit strong, I must admit. Embarrassing. Still, it was only her fun.'

'Fun! Dixie doesn't have an ounce of fun in her.'

'Anyway, you could be wrong about Dixie. You never can tell which way she will jump. She might be tickled pink with this place.'

'That'd be a laugh. Can you imagine Dixie queening it here, Perce? Hobnobbing with the gentry? If she gets ideas of anything like that she can give them up sharpish. I don't like to say this about my own daughter-in-law, but Dixie is common. Common as dirt. She's worse: she's blatant.'

'I know what you mean,' admitted the Earl. 'I have to admit that I prefer Dixie in small doses, though the kiddies are lovely kiddies, and always welcome. Still, Dixie won't worry us this weekend. There'll be all the others, and plenty of space to get away from her in, and the birthday party Saturday—we'll have too much to do to get annoyed by Dixie.'

'Dixie'll make herself felt.'

'Only if you let her, and get het up by her. Still, I admit it's a pity Phil couldn't be with her. Phil always seemed to dilute her, somehow.'

'He'll be out in three weeks,' said the Countess. 'It's something that she'll be visiting him tomorrow. He's had precious few visits from her while he's been in, that I do know. It'll probably put her in a foul mood. Those poor little mites . . .'

Her face softened at the thought of her grandchildren. Like most grandparents, she indulged the smallest ones of her family, the more so as she very seldom saw them.

'They need their dad,' agreed the Earl. 'It's been hard for them, him not being there. Still, one thing you've got to hand to Dixie; they're well-behaved.'

'Frightened out of their wits, more like.'

'No: be fair, Elsie. There's not many parents these days have the control over their kids that Dixie has.'

'Control's one thing, but I for one don't like to see kids too terrified to say a word when their mother's around. It's not natural. I know our kids weren't brought up like that.'

In silence they continued to gaze over the lustrous green and golden landscape, but their minds were far away from cows or haystacks. The thoughts of both of them were on their children and grandchildren, most of whom would be arriving the next day to celebrate the Earl's sixtieth birthday, his first in the state to which he had been called. Both of them were looking forward to the visit, as a relief from the grandiose monotony of Chetton Hall. But at the backs of their minds gnawings of doubt and uncertainty persisted. The Earl shifted from foot to foot, uneasily.

'It's a pity about Phil,' he said finally.

As always when the subject of her favourite child came up, the Countess raised her defensive prickles. Her mouth became set in a firm line.

'Phil was unlucky,' she pronounced. 'I've said it before, and I'll say it again. If there's any pity about Phil, it's that he married that Dixie. After they'd waited so long, too. You can dig a grave, but you don't have to jump straight into it yourself. But he's a good boy, Phil.'

'Easy-going,' agreed the Earl placatingly. 'Takes life as it comes. Never one to make trouble. Too much so, sometimes. That's how a type like Dixie can get the upper hand. But he's popular, that nobody can deny. I bet he's well liked where he is. And you could say the same about Trevor, in a way.'

'Ye-e-es,' said the Countess, more dubiously. 'In a different sort of way.'

Their eyes were taking in the trees of the Countess's Mile, their leaves just beginning to lose the brilliant green of spring, but their minds were contemplating the figure of their younger son.

'If anybody deserved to go to gaol it's Trevor,' said the Earl, without rancour. 'By gum! — he sails close to the wind sometimes. The sums he's had off the social security people — just lies barefaced and they believe him.'

'I hate to think what would happen if full employment came back,' said the Countess. 'He wouldn't know what to do with himself. Not that he doesn't make money, now and then. But I wouldn't call what he does *work*.'

'More like a sideline. To the social security.'

'It's embarrassing,' protested the Countess. 'Downright embarrassing. I wouldn't know where to look if the neighbourhood found out.'

'You can bet your bottom dollar they know,' said her husband. 'Trevor's name cropped up in the Prince Leopold just a day or two before all this landed on our plates, and old Fred Jarvis winked at me and nudged me in the ribs. Cheeky old sod! He's just the sort to go to these cinema clubs where they show that kind of stuff. You can bank on old Fred having put it all around Clapham by now.'

The Countess sighed.

'I don't know how I'll look the neighbours in the face, though Trevor doesn't seem to have any sense of shame. And this girl he's bringing with him, this Michele: she must be a right one if she appears in those pictures. First Prince Andrew, now our Trevor . . . She looked like the sort with only one thing on her mind.'

'Sex?'

'Number one. And willing to use whatever she's got to advance it. Bloody cheek, really, isn't it, Trevor inviting her along without so much as a by-your-leave, when we'd only met the girl for five minutes. Not to mention Dixie calmly announcing that she'd bring Chokey along.'

'That's different, Elsie. Chokey'll have been visiting Phil. That'll buck him up no end. They're pals.'

'Funny sort of pal. It was Chokey landed him in.'

'Now that's nonsense, Elsie. I know that's not how Phil sees it, and Chokey'll always be welcome as Phil's friend. It's not as though we haven't got room. We could lodge the whole Eighth Army here and there'd still be beds to spare. At least Joan and Digby won't be bringing anyone along with them.'

'No,' admitted the Countess. 'That wouldn't be Joan's way at all.'

'There's one of our children we don't have to make apologies for,' said the Earl, with a somewhat insecure heartiness. 'Hard little worker. Really got ahead. Set herself a goal, and achieved it. They're a lovely young couple.'

There was silence in the Green Drawing-Room.

'It's funny,' said the Countess at last, 'but I could never

really take to our Joanie. I tried, but I couldn't. They say it's sometimes like that with mother and daughter. I don't know if it was me or her, but I think it was her. There's something . . . I dunno . . . petty about her. Something mean-minded.'

The Earl, who was a kind-hearted man and an affectionate father, felt impelled to enter a protest.

'Come off it, Mother: Joan's just got her standards.'

'Oh yes — and doesn't she let everyone know it. I get fed up with her bleeding standards. Do you know, the last time I visited her — *by* invitation, as usual! — I was coming home on the bus, and there were these two women behind me, talking about one of the teachers at the local Junior School, and how fussy she was, and how she went on and on about the kiddies washing their hands after they'd been to the lav. And I sat there thinking: I bet that's our Joan. And it was! They said her name: Mrs Ferguson, they said. I could have sunk through the floor! Isn't that just like our Joan, getting all het up about a little thing like that?'

'She always was a clean little girl, I remember,' said the Earl. 'Fastidious, like.'

'You could call it that. Fussy's my word for it. She didn't get it from me. I'm not pernickety, and I'm not houseproud. She drives me up the wall the way she goes on when she comes round to us.'

The Countess turned from the window, and for the first time she surveyed the Green Drawing-Room with something approaching satisfaction.

'She'll have her work cut out if she's going to draw her finger along all the dust there is in *this* mauso-bloody-leum. I'll just hand her a duster and I'll say: "You get to it, my girl, and I'll see you next Christmas twelvemonth." '

'She does overdo it,' admitted the Earl, grinning at his wife's retreating back as she waddled back to the sofa and

took up her knitting. 'And Digby is a bit the same. Neat.
Precise. They're well matched, really. You can't imagine
Digby without a tie on or a handkerchief in his top
pocket, any more than you can imagine Joanie going
round with her hair in curlers. Still, you've got to
remember his job. You have to keep up a good
appearance in the insurance business.'

'You don't have to be prissy. And I'd call Digby prissy.'

The Earl turned back to the window, and gazed once
more at the cows, flicking their tails at the flies in the
Long Meadow.

'You don't think we went wrong with our kids somewhere, do you, Elsie?' asked the Earl.

CHAPTER 2

THE COUNTESS'S MILE

If the twelfth Earl of Ellesmere ever felt a sense of history
and of his place in it, it was not as a rule in the
magnificent residence of his family, whose splendour
overawed him and whose distances tired him. It came to
him, if at all, out of doors, perhaps when surveying the
acre upon acre of his fiefdom, perhaps when walking in
the cool reaches of the Countess's Mile. Sometimes in the
early morning, when he had made a pot of tea for himself
and his wife, had trailed it from the servants' hall, down
corridors endlessly winding, across the Great Entrance
Hall, up Sir Philip's Staircase, and down the narrow
domestics' passage that led him finally to the State
Bedroom—after all this (which was a continuation of a
duty regularly undertaken at Clapham, where it involved
perhaps one-tenth of the labour) he would often calm his
nerves with a stroll in the morning cool. And along the

Countess's Mile he would sometimes experience some lift of the soul, some message from the ethos of the place, that would make him pause in his track, put his hand on the trunk of an elm, gaze through the trees and across the Long Meadow towards Chetton Lacey, and say to himself:

'By Jove! These trees have been here hundreds of years. As long as my family has. It makes you think.'

In this the twelfth Earl was quite mistaken, for the elms of the Countess's Mile had been replanted shortly before the First World War. It was not these trees under which the fourth Earl's wife had flirted with Richard Mont, her groom, tapping him playfully with her whip as they swapped innuendoes drawn from the world of horsemanship; nor was it these that had seen the fourth Earl burst in on them and commence that ferocious attack on Richard Mont that had led to his serving three years for felonious assault in the most luxurious apartments in Newgate Prison. But the accuracy of the twelfth Earl's reflections is beside the point, for the Romantic impulse which led to that lift of the heart was of a kind that has never depended on literal truth. The important point was that it was there, even if it did not go very deep, and his man of business could not have caught him in a better place for his purposes, had he but known it, and had he but known how to make use of it.

But he did not. When Mr Lillywaite was sent thither by the Countess (in an early morning dishabille that was by no means as enticing as that of the first Earl's wife in the portrait by Kneller that dominated the Great Entrance Hall) he merely clicked his tongue at the unbusinesslike character of the place of meeting, and set reluctantly off.

When the Earl saw the cadaverous figure of his man of affairs approaching down the great flight of steps from the Dutch Garden, he roused himself from his mild reverie among times past and strolled to meet him along

the leafy shadows of the Mile, his mouth set in a genial
smile that involved him in some effort, for Mr. Lillywaite
did not inspire geniality.

'Lovely day, eh?' called the Earl. 'Makes you feel more
alive, a day like this. I always love walking down Clapham
High if there's early morning sunshine. Shall we take a
turn along the avenue here?'

The sunken face of the tall lawyer looked down into the
round face of the dumpy peer, and rather bleakly said:

'Of course. If you wish.'

Mr Lillywaite had long ago given up any attempt to
'My Lord' or even 'Sir' the present Earl, faced with the
crude ridicule that these formalities excited. Indeed, the
whole six weeks of their acquaintanceship had been one
series of shocks to Mr. Lillywaite's old-fashioned
sensibilities, beginning with the new Earl's demand that
before he and the Countess come to Chetton his man of
business should get rid of every man jack (and every
woman jill) of the house's domestic staff. 'Give 'em their
marching orders pronto,' the Earl had said. 'Me and Elsie
don't want spies around us all the time. We're not used to
it. And specially we don't want any of the toffee-nosed
types you get in these places, watching our every move.'
Mr Lillywaite (inspired by notions of decorum rather
than of humanity) had protested the length of service, the
devotion to the family, of this or that retainer,
but—beyond paying the severance pay that the law
demanded, and a very little over—the Earl had been
adamant. Mr Lillywaite had known from this point that
things were not going to go well, and they had not.

'Well,' he said now, gazing unhappily at his black
shoes, which were gaining a patina of sandy dust from the
surface of the Mile, 'we are getting on. There is clearly
going to be no difficulty in establishing your title, or
indeed your claim to the estate. There is no question that
your father's marriage to your mother was legal, and none

of any previous tie on either side.'

'I should think not,' said the Earl, with a touch of mustard in his tone. 'They were practically teenagers at the time, weren't they? He was just twenty, and Ma was eighteen and a bit, that's what I heard. It wasn't likely either of them had ever been spliced before.'

'No. No indeed. The marriage was always recognized by the family, even though, as you no doubt know, it was highly disapproved of.'

'They were too young. I don't wonder the family were against it.'

'That was one of their objections,' said Mr Lillywaite, from a great mental distance. The Earl shot him a quick glance that, had it been seen, might have warned Mr Lillywaite that he should not underestimate either the Earl's intelligence or his strength of character.

'Oh, I get the point,' said the Earl. 'I know they thought Ma wasn't their class. You don't have to be shy of saying it straight out. She wasn't either. I know that. But you could say we had the last laugh there, couldn't you?'

Mr Lillywaite sighed. Indeed you could. It was something that had not been foreseen. Even the old Earl — a courteous, prudent, private sort of man, an aristocrat of an old-fashioned school — had not foreseen it. He had settled the estate and the bulk of the family fortune on his grandson some years before, his only son being many years dead. The grandson had legally come into the estate on his coming of age, but it had been little more than a formal assumption. Who could have guessed that three weeks after the death of the old Earl, the young Earl would also die — driving up the M1, considerably inebriated, on the way from one celebration of his new independence to another, from one set of well-heeled drinking pals to another. It had all been unimaginably shocking to Mr Lillywaite's nervous system.

'The old Earl was, alas, never reconciled to his

brother,' went on Mr Lillywaite, in a well-practised voice of formal regret. 'This perhaps explains why he never cared to anticipate the possibility of — of *this* happening.'

'I'm surprised they never made it up,' said the Earl. 'After all, the marriage only lasted a year or two. I was hardly crawling when Dad left. Packed his bags and took ship to Australia. I believe he made good there: they say he ended up as a member of the South Australian parliament.'

Mr. Lillywaite's upper lip held the suspicion of a curl. That was not his idea of making good.

'Ye-es,' he said. 'Well, as I say, there can be no doubt that, on your father's death three years ago, you became the legal heir after the Earl's grandson. Naturally no arrangements to circumvent death duties could be made. There was every reason to assume that the young Earl would have heirs.'

'So I've heard,' said the Earl cheerfully, without any suspicion of disapproval. 'Sowed a fair few wild oats, from what we heard down at the local the other night.'

The idea of the Earl discussing his predecessor in a public house in Chetton Lacey was intensely distasteful to Mr Lillywaite. He would like to have made this clear to the Earl, but could think of no way that was likely to get through to him. After a pause he resumed the walk, the two of them resembling more and more a Victorian private tutor hired to rein in the levity and trivial-mindedness of a high-spirited young charge.

'Nevertheless, there is no question of any legal heir to the young Earl being in existence. So perhaps we could turn now to the question of the house. I trust you have turned the subject over in your mind since our last conversation?'

'Oh, I have,' said the Earl, walking confidently, even cockily forward, his hands clasped behind his back, looking very much as Harold Wilson used to look after a particularly triumphant Question Time in the House. 'The result is exactly the same. Elsie and me have made up our minds, and we're not going to go back on it. Sell out and get out. House, pictures, furniture—the lot. Get what they'll fetch is all we ask. We want to be rid of the whole caboodle.'

'Oh dear, oh dear, oh dear,' sighed Mr Lillywaite, his whole gaunt frame suggesting the stiffest form of disapproval. 'I must ask you—er, My Lord—to think what you are doing, think what this must do to the good name of the family in the eyes of the public at large. I have tried to make it as clear as I could that Chetton Hall and its contents are, considered as an entity, one of the national treasures.'

'Let the bleeding nation buy it, then—provided it pays the market price.'

Once more Mr Lillywaite, in spite of his natural servility, could not keep from his face a fleeting expression of distaste. He had always known that the old Earl's brother had married beneath him. The moment he heard, with horror, of the young Earl's death he had realized that the new Earl and his Countess might not be up to par. Quite how stupendously below par they would turn out to be he had not for a moment suspected.

'The point I tried to make at our last meeting,' he said, with what he felt was heroic patience, 'was that in these matters there is something more to be considered, something more than mere money. There are the family obligations, as custodians over the centuries of part of the nation's artistic and architectural heritage. This is one part—*one* part, only—of what we understand by the phrase *noblesse oblige*. It is this obligation that noble families like your own strive to uphold in these admittedly difficult times.'

'Not all of them they don't,' returned the Earl triumphantly. 'Do you think I haven't read in the papers about

that lot that live in the South of France and are selling the
old 'ome bit by bit and living off the proceeds like pigs in
clover? And I don't blame 'em either. The nation can't
have it both ways: you can't slam on death duties and
income tax and wealth tax and I don't know what, and
then scream 'noblesser bleege' when the people who've got
the stuff want to cash in their chips and get what they can
while the going's good.'

'Of course we would not disagree about death duties—'

'I'm damn sure we wouldn't. And another thing: when
you talk about "the national heritage" and all that rot,
how come this place was only open to the public one day a
year in the old Earl's time, eh?'

'Er . . . the old Earl felt . . .'

'Well now, I'm going to hand it to you straight: this is
one nobless that isn't going to bleege. I don't owe no
favours to the Chancellor of the Exchequer, nor to the
nation. Neither the one nor the other has ever done any
great favour to me. I'll be forking out enough from this
little lot as it is.'

'True, I can't deny it. There is, of course, the option of
offering Chetton to the National Trust,' murmured Mr
Lillywaite, following that line of thought reluctantly. 'But
I'm afraid that, even were you to do that, you would also
have to offer it a considerable sum to cover the upkeep.'

The Earl stared at him in disbelief.

'You must be joking.'

The lawyer did not pursue that option.

'I suppose,' he said, 'it will be necessary to offer the
nation certain works of art, in lieu of death duties.'

The Earl looked suspicious.

'Does that mean they'll be getting them on the cheap?'

'As a rule the sum agreed is rather less than the piece
would fetch on the open market.'

'Forget it. Sell to the highest bidder, and *then* pay the
death duties.' The Earl stopped in his tracks. Talk with

Mr Lillywaite always made him feel 'badgered'. He had felt the same way, not long before, when he had been questioned after a road accident by the police. It brought out all his usually latent aggression and pig-headedness. 'Here,' he said, turning to the lawyer with a look of intense suspicion on his face, 'you're not in the pay of the Chancellor or something, are you?'

Mr Lillywaite screwed up his face in an expression of pain and outrage, as if he had been accused of frequenting a credit-card brothel.

'Lord Ellesmere, I am merely trying to serve you — and the good name of your family — as best I can, in difficult circumstances. As I have done, and my father before me, all our working lives.'

'Okay,' said the Earl, speedily appeased, and equably resuming his walk, 'no offence. But from now on I'd be happier if you served me and let the family's good name take care of itself. The family's never done anything for me, you know.'

'Very well,' said Mr Lillywaite, also resuming his walk, but engineering a turn in the direction of the great house, conceivably hoping for some psychological effect from the sight of it. 'But you must realize that, even were selling decided on —'

'It is.'

'— it would be far from easy to find a buyer for a mansion — one might say a palace — of this size.'

'Don't you believe it. All these bleeding Arabs are just itching to buy up places like this. They point their prayer mats towards Buckingham Palace and pray it comes on the market.'

'But surely you wouldn't want —'

'I wouldn't give a monkey's fart.'

'For the neighbourhood it would be a sad, sad blow.'

'Don't you believe it. They'd lap it up. He'd come into residence once a year, throw open the grounds for a

church bazaar, wander round in his nightshirt and hand
out tenners for a slice of homemade sponge, and if I know
that bunch down at the Chetton Arms they'd love every
minute of it. They'd rake in a lot more shekels from Sheik
Yerfanny than they would out of me and Elsie. More than
they got out of the old Earl, too, I'd lay a tanner.'

'Hmm,' said Mr Lillywaite, unwilling to admit that the
Earl probably understood more about popular local
reaction than he himself did. If he had been unbiased,
which he was not, he would have admitted that the Earl
gave his opinions with a good deal of force, and that they
held more than a few grains of common sense. Indeed,
down at his real local, the Prince Leopold in Clapham,
the Earl's opinions on anything under the sun were
listened to by the regulars with the sort of respect they
gave the Prime Minister, appearing on the Jimmy Young
Show. But Mr Lillywaite was not yet willing to admit that
he had lost the argument.

'Of course, if any decision *were* made to sell, it ought to
be the decision of the whole family. You have to
remember that in this matter I in some sense represent
Lord Portsea's interests as well.'

'Whose? Oh — Phil's.'

'Your elder son's.'

'Oh well, Phil will be easy. He'll go along with anything
I decide. He's a good chap — never the sort to make
trouble. You'd like Phil. I'll introduce you when he gets
out.'

Mr. Lillywaite's eyebrows rose a fraction, but he had an
inkling he had discovered a straw worth clutching on to.

'These are, you realize, things that both he and *his*
heirs in their turn are vitally concerned in. Do I gather
you have not discussed them with him yet?'

'No, I haven't. Quite apart from the fact that discussion with Phil isn't that easy at the moment, I never
thought of it. I didn't discuss it with him when we sold the

house in Hackney and bought the house in Clapham, and I shan't discuss it with him when I sell this place neither. He wouldn't expect it.'

'Nevertheless, he has his rights. As heir presumptive he has clearly defined rights. I think it might be as well if I talked to him. You have no objections?'

'None at all. Visiting days are Mondays and Thursdays.'

'I feel sure the governor of Daintree will admit me whenever I care to appoint a time,' said Mr Lillywaite stiffly.

'Pals, eh? Yes, well, it's quite convenient Daintree being only thirty-five miles away. Dixie was going yesterday, then stopping the night in Bristol and coming on here this morning.'

'Ah — Lady Portsea.'

'That's the ticket. Mind you, Dixie is another type again. A mind of her own, has Dixie. Too much so, if you believe my Elsie. Philip'll go along with anything — happy-go-lucky type, open as the day is long. But you never know with Dixie — I haven't the faintest idea how she's taking all this.'

Lady Portsea's reactions to 'all this' did not interest Mr. Lillywaite. He had no curiosity about human feelings. He had never inquired about the present Earl's reactions on succeeding. He would have shrunk from the Earl's cliché — 'you could have knocked me down with a feather', as like as not — though he had accepted a whole barrage of clichés from the old Earl in his time, most of them to the effect that such and such behaviour was 'frightfully bad form', or that the country was 'going to the dogs' and its working men 'needed a good kick up the backside'. But though Mr Lillywaite did not speculate about the reactions of the new Lord and Lady Portsea, he did consider them, coolly, as possible new counters to be used on his side of the game.

'Well, that's all settled, then,' said the Earl. 'You know, I don't plan to stop here much longer. There's nothing to keep us, thank the Lord. You go and talk to Phil, but you'll find he certainly won't stand in our way. And I wouldn't take a blind bit of notice if he did. It's "Home, Sweet Home" for Elsie and me, and I tell you it's not a moment too soon. I always sleep light, but this business has been that much worry that I haven't had a good night's kip since we got to this place.'

'Certainly I'll see Lord Portsea as soon as I can make arrangements,' murmured Mr Lillywaite pensively.

They were emerging now from the Mile, and Mr Lillywaite noticed with regret that the Earl cast not a second glance at the monumental pile of Chetton Hall that now stood in all its glory before them. They strolled on, an ill-assorted pair, and they had just reached the flagged floor around the fountain when Mr Lillywaite paused, puzzled. From the distance, from behind his back in fact, there came the sound of a motor vehicle. Approaching nearer. Surely it could not be . . .

But he turned and — yes, it was. A vehicle — an estate car — was actually driving up the Countess's Mile, throwing up clouds of sandy dust in its wake.

'Dear God!' breathed Mr Lillywaite. 'Does this mean the reporters are on to this at last?'

But as he spoke the car emerged from the Mile and drew up beside them — actually drew up beside the splendid fountain designed by Auriol Jukes for the second Earl. The front window of the car was down, and from the driver's side emerged the head and shoulders of a heavily built and heavily made-up woman, with partially blonded hair and false eyelashes. She smiled a smile that was meant to be jovial but turned out to be ferocious, and waved a plump arm in the direction of the house.

'Hey, Dad, is it semi-detached or detached?' she yelled, and let out a yelp of laughter in self-congratulation at her wit.

'Get out, you lot,' she shouted over her shoulder, and the back opened and a quartet of children began to jump stiffly down. The driver's door opened briskly and the woman herself emerged. Her imposing bust was draped with a pink nylon blouse, and across her large hind-quarters were stretched a pair of brilliant orange slacks.

'What a place, eh, Dad?' she shouted, against the waters of the fountain, once more with that ferocious joviality. 'What rent's the Council rushing you for this little lot, then? It's a real giggle, isn't it: you and Elsie all on your tod in this great barn.' She turned to the figures emerging from the front part of the car. 'Chokey came with us to visit Phil. And you remember Sam, don't you, Dad? We won't interrupt.'

And smiling a wide, ingratiating smile in the direction of Mr Lillywaite, she marched up the steps to the Dutch Garden, in the wake of her children who had scampered up before and were now gazing raptly at the great house.

'Take your fingers off that flower, Karen. You pick that and I'll scalp you. Pull your bleeding socks up, for Christ's sake, Gareth. You're mixing with the gentry now.'

And the orange slacks proceeded in the direction of the Queen's Entrance, followed more slowly by one middle-aged man of watery eye and distinctly unreliable appear-ance, and by a large and amiable young West Indian. Even when she disappeared from view, her voice could be heard, shouting instructions to the children and accompanying them with threats of dire repercussions.

'Get along in, you lot, and if one of you puts smudges over the furniture, I'll have the hides off the lot of you — got that?'

Finally, as the two men stood there, the voice faded
into the distance, and it all seemed very quiet.

'That was Dixie,' said the twelfth Earl.

CHAPTER 3

SIR PHILIP'S STAIRCASE

The normal mode of approach to Chetton Hall was
through the main gates, past the lodge, then along a drive
of over a mile, past the Dower House, then finally into a
courtyard formed in the right-angle where the Blenheim
Wing intersects with the original house. Here steps would
be found leading to the Great Entrance Hall (for the
imposing Queen's Entrance on the West Front led to
nothing more than a dingy ante-room, whatever it may
have opened up to in the Danish Queen's time). In the
courtyard and the lawns around it, making no impact on
their manifest need for gardeners' attention, the Earl
pottered on the afternoon of his family's arrival, trying to
conceal a broad grin at the humour of it all. Friday
afternoon was well advanced before Joan and Digby drove
carefully into the courtyard and parked the car neatly
and unobtrusively under the windows of the Blenheim
Wing. Joan got out first, closed the door carefully, patted
at the creases in her skirt, then finally looked around at
the time-mellowed brick glories of the Jacobean house,
and the more stately splendour of the wing, executed by
Leoni in the early years of George I's reign.

'Very nice, Dad,' she said, and set her mouth into a
self-satisfied smile of the kind that was habitual to her.

The Earl kissed her, roaring with delighted laughter.

'That's the understatement of the year!' he shouted.

'Sounds as if you were visiting us in our retirement bungalow!'

'Actually, Dad, it's not any great surprise,' said Digby, emerging from the car and proving that it was possible to drive all the way from Wandsworth to Chetton without rumpling your natty pinstripe suiting. Joan wore a navy skirt and a frilly blouse that did nothing to disguise her incipient dumpiness; Digby was grey-suited, taller, with a boring little brown moustache and an irritating air of knowing rather more than the next man. 'We've been doing our homework on Chetton, Joan and I. Getting books out of the library. It's a famous house, you know: there are several books on it. So we knew exactly what it would be like, didn't we, Joan?'

'Oh yes,' said his wife calmly. 'It's so lovely. I do think you and Mum are privileged, just to have lived here for a while.'

'That's not how your mum looks at it, I can tell you. You should hear her on the subject. Which you probably will—here she comes.'

The Countess had been passing through the Great Entrance Hall and had seen the car through the open door, otherwise she very likely would not have exerted herself to greet her daughter. As it was, however, she waddled through the massive double doors, down the steps, and over to the car.

'Hello, Joanie,' she said.

'Hello, Mum,' said Joan, pecking her cheek.

It was a very English family reunion.

'Did you have a good trip down?' Lord Ellesmere asked Digby, who was busy humping from the boot of the car enough suitcases for a fortnight's stay at least.

'Absolutely splendid!' he said, with an enthusiasm unusual for him. 'And then the sight of the house from the road, and to see the Countess's Mile—'

'Knows the place already,' muttered the Countess.

'—just as we'd seen it in books—fantastically exciting. You've no idea how we've been looking forward to this.'

'Oh well, no accounting for tastes,' said the Countess disparagingly, as they turned towards the East door. 'I know there *are* people who go for this sort of thing, but give me the Ideal Home Exhibition any day. I tell you, Joanie, you're going to have to muck in and help with the cooking—you and Dixie and that other one. I'm doing a turkey for tonight, because you'll need something after the travelling, but I'm not slaving away over a hot stove all the bleeding weekend, not on your life.'

'Of course I'll give you a hand, Mum,' said Joan, with a bright smile. 'I'll enjoy it. I bet the kitchens are fabulous.'

The Countess emitted a bitter laugh.

'Ha! Wait till you see, my girl. Chamber of Horrors isn't in it!'

'I'm doing the stuffing,' said the Earl, trotting along beside them, and up the steps to usher them in. 'I'm proud of my stuffing. And I'll get a few bottles up from the cellar.'

'Better than you'd pick up at the off-licence, I bet,' said Digby. But they had passed into the Great Hall, and Digby suddenly caught his breath, put down the cases, and with a low whistle looked at the oak-panelled magnificence of it, and up the confident sweep of Sir Philip's Staircase.

'Like it, eh?' asked the Earl, with puppyish pleasure. 'Why don't you look around the house while your mum and I are busy? If you find a bedroom with a bed made up, just plonk yourselves down and call it your own.'

'We'd like that,' said Joan.

'Make yourselves at home, as far as you can in this great hole,' said the Countess. 'Trevor and that creature he's brought with him have already. Found a room with a lot of jazz records in, and they're up there playing Felonious Monk or something.'

Digby cast a look of covert contempt at the retreating backs of his noble mother and father-in-law, and then— without speaking, but with a quick look at each other—he and his wife separated and began to prowl around the Great Hall, gazing intently at everything there was to see. To the casual eye they might have seemed no different from the tourists who came to the house on the rare days when it was open to the public: she earnestly intent on taking in everything, he with his more casual glances, designed to suggest effortless discrimination. But a closer attention might have marked them off from the usual tourist or tripper, for in both their eyes there was a sharp glint—of intelligence, of cupidity, of an unusual kind of lust. And as they neared the door of the Dining-Room, and were about to go through, Digby lightly touched Joan on the arm and gestured towards an object in the shadows beside the foot of the great staircase.

'Bernini,' he whispered. 'One like that went at Sotheby's last month. Fetched sixty thou.'

Joan's eyes became round as saucers. And together they went through the door and admired the superb but less portable Grinling Gibbons carvings round the portrait panel over the fireplace.

'That would have to stay,' said Digby regretfully.

Digby and Joan could not have known it, for Chetton is a huge house, but in another part of the Hall, in the Long Gallery that opened off from the stairwell, Dixie's friend Chokey was engaged in a comparable assessment of the house's contents. Chokey was fiftyish, slightly grubby, his considerable bulk enclosed in loose, cheap, brown suiting. Chokey's eyes were watery but cunning, but since he very seldom looked at anyone he was talking to they were not often remarked on. From time to time in his progress along the gallery Chokey placed nicotine-stained fingers on the frame of a picture, or on a marble bust.

Chokey was much less subtle than Digby and Joan, and nobody who watched him would have been in any doubt that, like them, he was pricing things, though he probably had in mind considerably less reputable outlets for the objects he was pricing.

In fact, Chetton Hall was so large—practically, as Mr Lillywaite had said, a palace—that all the Spenders and their friends could settle themselves in and look around and yet be quite unaware of each other. In the suite of rooms that had been the young Earl's in the lifetime of his grandfather, the present Earl's younger son Trevor had made himself at home, and so had his current girlfriend. Trevor was fair, slim, with an expression on his mildly good-looking face of weak goodwill, which might only become operative under stress. Michele was dark, with a lithe, slim body—they would have gone well together horizontal in cinemascope—but her mouth was hard and her eye determined. Trevor, it would have needed little perspicacity to guess, would at a crunch be putty in her hands.

The pair had been at Chetton several hours, and, wearying of the Countess's doom-ridden disapproval, they had early on discovered the young Earl's suite. They had lighted on a cabinet of jazz records, as well as a wardrobe of fascinating clothes, a bed with green silk sheets, a silver casket of odd-flavoured cigarettes, a private bar, and a stock of contraceptive equipment for emergencies—not that Trevor or Michele were ever caught out unprepared. All in all, the young Earl's suite gave the pair a definite feeling that this house was something.

'It reminds me,' said Michele, gazing up at the elaborate raised design of the ceiling, 'of the house we used when we made *Evie and the Mad Marquis*. Sort of derelict manor it was—Dorset, or Devon, or somewhere—and we more or less commandeered it, you know: film was finished before they knew we were there. You weren't in that, were you?'

'No, before my time,' said Trevor, getting out of bed and fetching himself a cigarette. 'Was it any good?'

'Usual stuff,' said Michele, resting her dark head against the green pillow and screwing her mouth into a pout of boredom. 'Usual stuff, only with a lot of whips and branding-irons and things. They used harpsichords and that in the background, to get in the class customer. The sado stuff attracts the class, as a rule. I say, you don't half look sexy with that black cigarette, and all naked on the green sheets. Some director ought to use that.'

'I look sexy with my clothes on,' said Trevor. 'Nobody's ever given me a chance to show it.'

'Trevor,' said Michele pensively, 'have you ever thought what difference all this will make to your career?'

'I'm not sure I have a career. What do you mean?'

'I mean you having a title and that. It gives you a certain cash-ay, you know. If you could capitalize on it, it could do a lot for you — get you bigger parts and all. We could move into the big time together.'

'I'm not sure I have a title,' said Trevor. 'And I wouldn't have thought it was much of a qualification for our kind of film. Talking of which, I'm feeling sexy again. Didn't know I had it in me, not without the cameras being there. Must be the sheets. So if you —'

But his eye caught something outside the window, and he hopped out of bed to take a look.

'Lumme, look at that,' he said. Michele swanned out from between the sheets in a practised way, and together they stood at the window as if posing for an artistic shot for *The Naturist*. Down below in the Long Meadow a black man was walking among the cows, taking shot after shot of the matchless West Front of Chetton with expensive photographic equipment. From time to time he would turn round, and take close-ups of the cows, who

clearly regarded him as an interesting variation on the
monotony of their daily routine. Finally, when he had
taken enough photographs, he turned his attention
wholly to them, patting their necks, pretending to ride
them, and finally throwing himself into a crazy dance in
and around the beasts, his feet making frenzied patterns
among the daisies, his hands clapping over his head. He
laughed and cried out, and the cows stood regarding him
in intense absorption.

'It's that spade of Dixie's,' said Trevor. 'Lives down the
street from us. She sure knows how to pick 'em.'

'It reminds me of *Caribbean Orgy*,' said Michele.
'There was this scene—'

'I know. I was in it,' said Trevor. 'All blacked up. Come
on, I'll put on a Johnny Dankworth and we'll go back to
bed.'

'Regard it,' said Michele, 'as a rehearsal. For our future
in the big time.'

A couple of hundred yards down the corridor from this
paradisal couple, in the doorway of the State Bedroom,
where the Earl and Countess had settled, out of sheer
exhaustion, on their first arrival (it was the first bedroom
they had come to), four small figures were standing,
gazing at its faded, dusty immensity with eight large eyes.

'It's bigger than our whole house,' said Karen softly.

'No, it's not, silly,' said Gareth, the eldest. 'But it's very
big.'

'It's not big, it's eNORmous!' said Cliff, his voice rising.

'It's tremenjous!' yelled the littlest.

'Shhh!' hissed Karen. They all fell silent, then took
their heads out of the doorway and peered both ways
along the corridor.

'Where is she?'

'Who?' asked the baby, who did not yet know who 'she'
invariably was.

'Old Mother Slap,' said Cliff.

'Shhh,' said Karen again. She was a child who made nods at the conventions.

'The purple-toed monster from outer space,' said Gareth, who was not. 'She's not around. We'd have heard if she was. I expect she's yelling at those little boys on the fountain to pull their socks up.'

Karen giggled louder than anyone at this. Gareth pulled them all inside the room and, heaving somewhat, closed the door. It seemed to act as a signal. All three older children flung themselves on each other with Red Indian whoops, and in an ecstasy of liberation began fighting all over the floor. The smallest chortled with joy, and joined in to the limits of his strength by gamely tugging at any shoe or hand that projected itself from the *mêlée* of whirling bodies. The game lasted a delirious five minutes, for the children had a mighty load of energy to release. At the end Karen and Gareth extricated themselves, panting and laughing, and sat up to look around them again.

'I say,' said Gareth, 'do you realize—'

'Yes,' said Karen.

'What?' demanded the baby.

'That in a house this size,' said Karen, taking him on her knee, 'with all these thousands and thousands of rooms and corridors and things, we'd never have any trouble getting away from—from *her*.'

'From old Big Bum,' said Cliff.

'Cliff!' said Karen.

'From old Floppy Bos,' said Gareth.

'From the old witch!' screamed the baby.

'You are terrible,' said Karen. But she joined with all the rest, looking at each other, their eyes afire with wonder and surmise.

'Wouldn't it be just wonderful!' Karen said.

The children had been in error when they decided that
their mother could not be anywhere near them because
she could not be heard. She was, in fact, less than fifty
yards away, though she, in her turn, had heard nothing
of their uproar. She was standing at the top of Sir Philip's
Staircase, and was looking about her. She had changed
into a flouncy dress, three-quarter length, with a blue
and purple design and yards of gauzy drapes. She had
bought it to celebrate her last wedding anniversary and,
notwithstanding the inability of her husband to be with
her, she had celebrated regardless. Dixie had brought it
with her as the grandest thing she owned. She had
remade her face into a mask of pink, beige and black. She
was, for once, not in the middle of a whirl of noise and
activity. Leading off from the staircase was the Long
Gallery. Dixie gazed carefully down that — heavy with the
portraits of her husband's ancestors. Then she peered into
the murk of a stubby little corridor off to her left, then
down into the panelled dignity of the Great Hall. When
she was quite sure she was alone, she inspected the
carpeted expanse of the staircase, nodding as she counted
the steps. She squared her fine shoulders, fixed her eyes
straight ahead of her, and then, at first uncertainly, but
with growing expertise, began descending the stairs with
a step that could only be described as regal.

Anyone seeing her at that moment might well have
concluded that Lady Portsea was beginning to scent
enticing future possibilities.

'Turkey's sizzling,' said the Earl, rubbing his hands. 'If
you nip through the hall and half a mile down the
corridor to your left you might get a whiff. Blimey — think
of my lot never getting the smell of turkey in the oven.'

They had all gathered in the Dining-Room. The Earl
had stationed himself by the fireplace, under the portrait
of Sir Rupert Spender. His face was enclosed by the

riot of fruit and flowers within which Grinling Gibbons had enclosed the portrait, so that he looked like nothing so much as an amiable greengrocer peering out from among his wares. At his right hand, on the marble fireplace, he had placed an enormous can of beer.

'Anyone else feel like a snifter? I got a bumper keg of Watbread's Special from the local — I know Chokey won't say no to sharing it with me. But there's other stuff around too: part of the loot, you might say. What'll you all have?'

'I'll have a dry sherry, Dad, please,' said Joan.

'For me too,' said Digby.

'Have you got brandy and blackcurrant?' asked Michele.

'A gin and tonic, please, Dad,' said Dixie, patting at a flounce. Something in her tone led Joan to dart her a sharp glance.

But the Earl had held up his hand.

'Here — I can't remember all that! It's every man for himself. It's all in the cabinet through there in the lounge. Chokey, boy: here's a glass of your favourite.'

While the rest stampeded in the direction of the doors to the Green Drawing-Room, Chokey came forward and accepted the proffered glass of beer — a shade reluctantly, perhaps, as if he'd have preferred something a bit harder, but his watery, shifty eyes were fixed on the Earl's shoes, and he voiced profuse thanks.

'Sam?' said the Earl, holding out the bumper can.

'No, thanks, man,' said Sam, and strolled elegantly into the Green Drawing-Room and poured himself a neat cognac. Sipping it, Sam stood in the large open doorway that separated the two rooms, gazing silently around at the splendours of both. He and Chokey kept themselves somewhat apart — perhaps feeling themselves strangers at a family party, perhaps feeling (who knows?) that the Spenders' ennoblement had somehow marked them off.

Chokey lurked in a dark far corner, saying little to anyone, but, like Sam, looking around him a lot, and keeping his ears open.

'Well,' said the Earl, when they had gathered again. 'This is nice, I must say.'

'That's it, you see,' said the Countess to no one in particular, heaving her bulk into a gilded chair by the fireplace. 'This is how he would have it. But don't think you're going to eat here for the rest of the weekend. Not on your life. There's a great big table in the kitchen where the servants used to eat. We'll use that. Food'll be a sight hotter, that's for sure.'

'I thought we ought to do it once,' said the Earl, standing by his lady's side and surveying with some pride the table which it had taken them half an hour to lay. 'It's a sight, isn't it, eh? Like those old costume films with Margaret Lockwood your mum used to love. It's all part of the ancestral loot. Fancy some of the cut glassware, Joanie?'

Joan's eyes glinted, but the children claimed their grandfather's attention. They were ranged down the side of the table, clutching glasses with something orange in them, but gazing wide-eyed at the table, which was groaning under the weight of silver, glassware, candelabra and tureens that any museum in the country would have itched to get its fingers on. Karen lifted the littlest one up to see.

'I think it's lovely, Grandad,' she said.

'Who asked you?' snapped Dixie, in a semi-automatic response. She immediately tried to retrieve it, turning to the Earl and saying in a very different tone of voice: 'She's like that, though, Karen is. Loves to have things nice. Appreciates it.'

Once again Joan shot her a sharp glance, and Sam too, from his doorway, cast an amused look in her direction. For both of them had suddenly realized what had been bothering them about Dixie. She was attempting a refined accent. Apparently she was auditioning for the part of Lady of the Manor. The Earl, however, was oblivious.

'I know she does. She's a lovely girl, is my Karen. And take a good look, my little lady, because you won't be seeing this little lot every day of your life.'

Thus launched on to the subject closest to his heart, the Earl seemed inclined to open up to the family his whole thinking on the matter. He took a great gulp of his beer and set the glass down on the chimneypiece.

'Fact is, your mum and I hope to be out of all this in ten days or so — two weeks at the outside. Everything seems to be sorting itself out — quick as you can expect, anyway, with lawyers in the picture. So as soon as we can make it, we're going to pack our bags and make for home, and leave old Lillywaite to sell the place up.'

Nobody looked directly at anyone else, but Digby and Joan, who had had an earnest little conversation in the privacy of their bedroom, breathed tiny sighs of relief.

'So you're going to put the place on the market, are you, Dad?' Digby said. 'I think you're wise. It seems a terrible shame, but in the end it would only have been a millstone round your necks.'

'Nobody expected you to stop,' said Joan, who nevertheless did rather wish she could have had a longer and more complete initiation into gracious living while they were there. 'I wish you'd kept the staff on, though, Dad. You'd have been a lot more comfortable while you were here.'

'No fear,' said the Earl, looking more like Low's Little Man every minute. 'Not on your life. Of course the estate workers stayed on. Even I know the cows have to be milked. But having butlers and what-have-you watching our every move — that's not our style at all.'

'You'd have soon got used to it.'

'As the judge said when he sentenced the man to thirty years in the salt mines. No, ta very much: that's not something Elsie and I want to get used to. As I said to Lillywaite: we're not having spies around the house. Listening to every word we say. Watching. What the Butler Saw and all that. Not that there's much of *that* for him to see these days, eh, Elsie?'

The Earl let out a bellow of laughter, but his daughter flinched and pursed her lips, as she often did at the uninhibited animality of the children in her class. The Earl resumed his discourse.

'Anyway, even if we'd wanted to—*which* we don't, and never will—there's all them death duties to be paid off. My noble family couldn't go in for any of the regular dodges this time. The only sensible thing is: get what they'll fetch, pay over what's got to be paid, and make hay with the rest.'

His words fell on silence, as various little brains set to the calculation of their interests, the assessing of their positions.

'The death duties will be phenomenal, of course,' said Digby, whose brain was quicker by experience at this sort of calculation. 'But this stuff will fetch, make no mistake.' He waved his hand towards the picture over the fireplace above the Earl's head. 'That's a Van Dyke. That alone would fetch three-quarters of a million.'

'Oh, been pricing it, have you?' said the Countess nastily.

'Mum!' protested Joan. 'It's Digby's job. He is a valuer. Digby just knows these things.'

'Well, bully for Digby,' said the Countess. 'Any Van Dykes come up for sale in Wandsworth and Digby's the boy to call in.'

'Mother!' said the Earl. He turned round and gazed at the picture enclosed within the Gibbons carvings. It was of Sir Rupert Spender, grandfather of the first Earl, who had fought for King and Commonwealth (successively) in the Civil War, and whom a later portrait by Lely showed as one of those hard-faced men who do well out of wars. Here, however, he was in the prime of youth, his hand on the head of a pointer, his slim body clad in a blue velvet suit with lacy collar and cuffs.

'Three-quarters of a million, just for nancy boy here,' said the Earl. 'It makes you think.'

'Don't be nasty,' said Michele. 'I think he has a look of Trevor.'

They all looked at Trevor, then at the portrait of Sir Rupert, then back at Trevor. Certainly there was a resemblance: the same fair-brown hair, the same good-looking but slightly pinched face. The resemblance was accentuated by the velveteen jacket and floppy bow-tie that Trevor was wearing, filched from the wardrobe of *Evie in the Naughty Nineties*.

'Thank you, Michele,' said Trevor, enjoying the notice. 'There's my reputation gone. Only nancy roles for me from now on.'

Michele's remark had brought her to general notice. Joan, who had earlier cast glances of prim disapproval at the thin white shift which was apparently her sole garment, seemed suddenly seized by a desire to play the hostess. Perhaps she was spurred on by the fact that the Countess made no gestures at all in that direction, or perhaps she was just working towards an alliance of the family's younger members. She leaned forward to the slim girl, and with a condescending smile said:

'How clever of you to notice . . .er, Michele, is it?'

'Michele with one l,' said the girl, turning her hard eyes in Joan's direction.

'You must have a genius for faces,' said Digby, leaning forward in his turn. 'How did you first meet Trevor?'

'When he was shoved on top of me, on a bed, with arc lamps behind him,' said Michele. 'That way you never forget a face.' And then, turning to the assembled family, began: 'About Trevor: we've been talking about his career, and—'

But the Countess was having nothing of this, and heaved her bulk out of her chair like an ageing coalman.

'Well, no peace for the wicked. I'm going to serve up down there, and you can come and get it in ten minutes. You—whatsyername?—Sam: you look as if you could bring up three or four. And Chokey and Perce, you can bring up the rest.'

'The kids can fetch their own,' said Dixie. And in what passed with her for *sotto voce* added: 'And if any of you spill one drop of gravy on them Persian carpets . . .'

As the Countess waddled out, the Earl resumed his discourse, determined that his intentions should be entirely understood.

'No—as I say, it's sell out and get out. Sale of the century, everything must go. Old Lillywaite tried to bring Phil into it, but I said to him: "I wouldn't expect him to consult me if he was selling his house, and I won't be consulting him when I sell mine." '

'Still,' said Dixie, who had been very thoughtful in the last few minutes, since the Earl had started explaining his intentions, 'you could go and talk it over with Phil, Dad. It's not far, and he'd love to see you. And he is the heir.'

'Heir, my Aunt Fanny,' said Lord Ellesmere. 'That's one old Lillywaite tried to pull. I said to him—'

But he was interrupted by the telephone. He looked wildly round in several directions, trying to remember where the nearest extension was. Then he darted through the doors into the Green Drawing-Room and grabbed up the receiver.

'Hello, Mr Lillywaite. Talk of the . . . your name was on our lips.'

The phone was on a Chippendale side table on the wall near the door. Sam had moved away when the call came through, and the Earl now stood in the doorway, smirking at his children.

'Yes, thank you, Mr Lillywaite: Lady Joan has arrived . . . And the Honourable Trevor.'

'Whoops! There goes my reputation again,' said Trevor, giving his father a tremendous smirk in return. But Joan merely responded with a dignified smile. It was, after all, the first time she had heard the title used. She had had a vague feeling that it might have been abolished by the last Labour government.

'You've arranged to see Phil, have you? . . . Tomorrow afternoon? . . . Quite all right with me, mate . . . and with Dixie, I'm sure . . . She was just saying Phil enjoyed having visitors . . . Say "keep your chin up" from us, will you? And say we'll see him in three weeks' time, when he's out . . . Oh, and Lillywaite: it won't make a ha'porth of difference, you know.'

He put down the phone in high good humour, and came back into the Dining-Room, rubbing his hands.

'Never did like lawyers. He's batting on a sticky wicket if he thinks he can make trouble between Phil and me. Phil's a good lad.'

'Too bloody good, sometimes,' muttered Dixie to herself. But she turned to the Earl casually, and said: 'What did you say his name was, Dad?'

Joan looked down at her hands, and tightened her mouth.

'Lillywaite. Pompous old twerp he is too. Well, come on, Sam, come on, Chokey. Turkey up. You going to come and get yours, my little darlings?'

And the Earl and his helpers bustled off to the kitchen. In the Dining-Room a sudden hush fell, and then they all started making their way, awkwardly, to the table.

'Isn't it lovely?' said Dixie, in a voice that was most un-Dixie.

'Oh, look at that,' said Joan, vexed. 'They've got all the

knives and spoons the wrong way round.'

'Put us all right, then, Joanie,' shrilled Dixie, instantly her normal self. 'We didn't know you'd been in domestic service.'

Joan and Digby, both giving tense little smiles, went round the table from place to place, rearranging the cutlery. Then they stood back, hands clasped in front of them, and nodded in satisfaction.

'Isn't it marvellous?' muttered Dixie.

Then the turkey came in, Sam bearing four plates expertly in his big hands, the rest juggling them as they might. The children gazed at their plates, and then wide-eyed once more around the rose-papered room, with the immensely white table cloth and the sparkling glasses. Then the Earl dashed back to the kitchen and returned with three bottles of wine, followed by the Countess, who sank exhaustedly into her place without a word, conveying a distinct aura of reproach to them for the effort their coming had put her to. The Earl handed a bottle to Trevor, and one to Digby, and together they filled up the glasses, Digby covering the neck dexterously to prevent drips. Then the Earl stood at the foot of the table, stepped back to admire his handiwork and see that everyone was served, and then took up his glass.

'To the big Spenders,' he said.

CHAPTER 4

DAINTREE MANOR

The open prison where Philip, Lord Portsea, was spending the last few months of his four-year sentence for robbery was a collection of wooden huts clustered around a modest, early nineteenth-century manor house a few miles outside the village of Daintree, in Gloucestershire. In the Manor the Governor had his flat, the rest of the house being given over to recreation rooms and workshops that taught trades in anticipation of the inmates' release — weaving, basket-work and making paper hats for Christmas crackers, according to Lord Portsea in his one letter home since being transferred there. It was a moot point whether the Manor was colder than the huts, or the huts than the Manor, but in every other respect Daintree Open Prison was a relaxed and civilized place. So that, though it was not as open as its name implied, being surrounded by a wall, nevertheless the inmates, for whom the wall was child's play, never bothered to attempt a permanent escape. Why escape to the harsh economic realities of Thatcher's England, after all? Even the food at Daintree was good, being prepared by an Italian chef who had committed an act of violence on his wife's lover with a meat axe. So that, all in all, Phil was, as he said with a grin to Chokey during his recent visit, lucky to get in there.

But then, of course, everybody liked him, as the Earl had so confidently asserted that they must. Back in Maidstone, where he had served the first years of his sentence, he had regularly played dominoes with the Chief Warder, and the Governor had used his case as exemplary in a very civilized and forward-looking letter to the *Guardian*. The Governor thought that Phil should never have been in gaol in the first place, and the Governor of Daintree agreed with him.

The Countess's view, as we have seen, was that Phil had been unlucky. And of course it is unlucky if, when you are engaged in nicking a lorry-load of television sets, you happen to get caught red-handed by the police. Particularly as Phil had had three previous convictions for similar offences, when the judges, entranced by Phil's cheery openness and charm, had given exceptionally light sentences. The fourth judge was very old, and quite impervious to charm.

The Governor of Daintree had been most interested by his telephone conversation with Mr. Lillywaite. Rumours of Phil's new state had gone round the prison, especially since the somewhat spectacular incursion of Dixie and Chokey on Thursday. What had been lacking had been details. The Governor indicated that Mr Lillywaite would be at liberty to interview Lord Portsea at any time he cared to appoint; and he added that he, the Governor, would be most pleased to talk to Mr Lillywaite after he had finished his business. Mr. Lillywaite fixed the next day, the Saturday, and clicked his thanks into the phone. Then he sat back in the swivel chair of his dull little office in Chetton Lacey and thought deep thoughts.

The next day, after lunch, Mr Lillywaite drove himself to Daintree.

The Governor had considered making available for the interview a room in his own flat, but had decided that this might make him look ridiculous in the eyes of inmates and warders alike. He compromised by ordering that tea and cakes be served in the usual bare hut where the prisoners met their relatives, loved ones and associates. Mario the cook took this as permission to prepare a magnificent Neapolitan speciality of meringue-like consistency, one mouthful of which was enough to sate a normal stomach. Mario's tea, however, was English, and Mr Lillywaite and Phil enjoyed it as they conducted the preliminaries to the interview, and sized each other up.

Mr Lillywaite, like Phil's most recent judge, was impervious to charm, but he was not imperceptive of it. He registered it in Phil—ill-bred ragamuffin street charm, he called it in his own mind, but he admitted that it was there, and he allowed it to flow over him, so that, by degrees, he began to feel very much more at home with Lord Portsea than he did with his noble father. Phil was burly, with the beginnings of a paunch; his hands were large — workman's hands, but not very recently used — and his smile was utterly guileless. He would have made an expert salesman of vacuum cleaners, thought Mr Lillywaite: no housewife would have been able to resist him. He was also, if appearances were not deceptive, exceptionally easy-going. A man who went along with the crowd, a man whom it was all too easy to lead into dubious enterprises, since he'd do anything to help a pal. But Mr. Lillywaite did not allow this impression to gain too firm a foothold in his mind: he had not been in the law for thirty-five years without learning that appearances, particularly the appearances of criminals, are indeed all too frequently deceptive.

He had brought to the interview a magnificent coffee-table book about Chetton Hall and its park — its history, its inhabitants and its treasures — and as they talked and drank tea Lord Portsea leafed through it, casting intelligent and appreciative glances at the volume's lavish colour spreads.

'Blimey,' he said, as he surveyed a picture of the Long Gallery, 'the guv'nor's really landed in the soft seat, hasn't he?'

'Ye-es,' said Mr Lillywaite ingratiatingly. 'And that's really what I wanted to talk to you about.'

'Oh yes?' said Phil, somewhat perfunctorily. He had lighted on a double-page spread of the park, and he pursed his lips into a whistle. 'Just look at that! Hampstead Heath isn't in it!'

'It is indeed a splendid prospect,' agreed Mr Lillywaite, his voice becoming warmer. 'That was taken from the Green Drawing-Room. Snowdon, you know.'

Phil furrowed his brow as if looking for a mountain, and then said: "Oh, Princess Margaret's ex.'

'That's right. One of the finest views in England, that, in my opinion. Though of course I may be prejudiced:

you do understand my interest in this matter, Lord Portsea?'

Phil chuckled at the title and went on leafing through the pages of the book.

'You're the guv'nor's man of law,' he hazarded. 'Business manager, accountant, and all that malarkey.'

'Well, perhaps I do partake a little of all those functions,' said Mr Lillywaite, allowing himself a lawyerly little smile. 'But I like to think of myself as the servant of all the family, of the family as a whole. As indeed I have been for many years. Now, in the normal course of events, what I should be advising your father, the new Lord Ellesmere, to do at this moment would be to begin the process of transferring the bulk of the estate—land, house, contents and so on—to you, as a gift. And to begin it as soon as possible.'

'Oh yes?' said Phil, his attention at last distracted from the book.

'Yes. The purpose being, as I'm sure you will understand, to minimize death duties. Your father may have many years of active life ahead of him. Let us hope so. But still, he is a man of—'

'Sixty,' said Phil. 'Sixty today. The family will all be down at the house. They're going to have a bit of a knees-up tonight.'

'Ah yes, so I believe. Sixty. So he is far from being a young man. And the longer the time that elapses between the deed of gift and his death, the less you would pay.'

'I get you,' said Lord Portsea. And clearly he did. The book was forgotten and he was looking at the lawyer, his brow creased in thought. 'Seems a bit hard on the old 'uns, though, don't it? I mean, they no sooner come into a bloody great fortune than they have to hand it over again. I don't know what they want to do with it—holidays in the South o' France, new Mercedes, blow-up oyster and Guinness supper for the whole street—but I wouldn't blame them if they didn't want to give it all up, now they've just got their hands on it.'

'I assure you, Lord Portsea, that the Earl and Countess would be left with ample funds — ample to encompass not merely their needs, but anything they could possibly desire along the lines you suggest. But perhaps I should explain why I would give the Earl that advice. The landed families, in this century, have seen it as their duty to maintain the family heritage — in particular to ensure the future of it in the hands of the eldest son.'

'They see things rather differently in our neck of the woods,' said Phil.

'Inevitably — and quite rightly,' said Mr Lillywaite. 'When there is not the same question of maintaining a heritage intact.'

'What about Trevor and Joanie?'

'No doubt some more modest provision could be made for the younger children,' said the lawyer. 'Indeed, the first thing I did for the Earl when he succeeded was to draw up an emergency will along those lines, pending some more permanent arrangement.'

'I don't think I can quite see our Joan and her Digby being satisfied with a modest provision,' said Phil. 'She'll be getting ready to rake in her share, with Digby standing by, pocket calculator at the ready.'

'That may well be a danger,' said Mr Lillywaite, smiling once more his thin, ingratiating smile, as if he were entering a conspiracy with Phil. 'It frequently is with younger children. The problem here is that your father in his heart sympathizes. And if your father disperses the property by sale, there will be no argument against apportioning the family fortune in whatever manner he pleases.'

'So that's what Dad's out to do, is it?'

'Your father has decided to — I quote him — "sell out and get out". In which case, as I say, considerations of maintaining the family heritage in the hands of the eldest hardly apply any longer. Now, you can see, I'm sure, Lord Portsea, that in this matter I am the servant of your father (unless I decline to serve him in such a desecration of all I have striven to maintain, which may indeed be the case). But I am also, as I tried to convey to him, the servant of the family as a whole. I feel it my duty to warn you, therefore, that your own interests and those of your children could be very gravely damaged if the Earl were to continue in his present determination.'

Phil's face wore a look of unusual seriousness, and he got up and walked around the bare little room, finally landing up by the window. He looked out over the lawns of what once had been Daintree Manor, towards the other huts and the trees down by the stream. At last he turned round and looked once more at Mr Lillywaite.

'Meaning, in plain language,' he said, 'that in the normal course of events I might have expected the bulk of the loot to come straight to me.'

'Quite.'

'And after me, to Gareth.'

'Indeed, yes.'

'And that what Dad wants is to realize the cash, then split it into three or something, and—'

'I suspect that would be his instinct. He strikes me as a very fair man. And after all, if it is basically a question of mere money, why not? But the survival of our great families, as families, in the homes of their ancestors, has not been achieved by fairness. Quite the contrary.'

Phil sat down again and took up the book.

'And what you'd like to see is me and Dixie settling down—at Chetton, I mean—when I get out, which is only three weeks or so away, and setting ourselves up as Lord and Lady of the Manor?'

'Exactly. But my meaning is basically, Lord Portsea, that you would in fact run the family business, if I may so express it. I believe that even Her Majesty the Queen refers to her duties in those terms.'

'No kidding?'

'And the Spender family, I must remind you, has immense family interests. Even after the death duties that the present Earl must inevitably pay, a very great deal will remain. It might, I think, be necessary to open the house to the public . . .'

'I might enjoy that,' said Phil, with a chuckle.

'It would be a full-time occupation, for you and for your wife. But an immensely rewarding one. And you would be bringing your son up in the house that would one day be his.'

Phil sat forward in his hard wooden chair, his shoulders hunched in thought.

'The Press'd have a field day,' he said at last. 'Out of jug and into the stately pile.'

'The Press, as yet, have not got on to the story,' said Mr Lillywaite. 'And the Press can be dealt with by saying nothing whatever to them.'

'We must read different papers,' said Phil, still hunched forward in thought. 'Not that I'd mind the publicity. Bit of a giggle, really. What I don't like is this business of going against the guv'nor. I mean, if he wants to sell, that's his business, isn't it?'

'I have the impression,' said Mr Lillywaite, also in his turn leaning forward with an air of urgent sincerity—the more urgent because he was subtly adapting the truth, 'that what the Earl and Countess really want is to get away from Chetton and to go back home to . . . er . . . Clapham. Quite understandable, too. Laudable. They don't feel easy. They conceive that this would be the speediest means of accomplishing that end. But it might be achieved quite as readily by what I am proposing. They would go back home with a tidy income to keep them comfortable, but not so great a one as to embarrass

them, or to subject them to harrassment. The important
thing is, how best to approach them. I feel that if the
matter were put to them — by you, for example — in the
right manner . . .'

'If I put the pressure on, you mean?'

Mr Lillywaite pursed his lips with distaste.

'I have the impression that both your parents are
very fond of you. We need only talk about
pressure — emotional pressure, if you will — as a last
resort.'

'There's one thing you've forgotten,' said Phil, finally
straightening up. 'Dixie. Really it all depends on Dixie.'

Lord Portsea fumbled in his pocket and brought out a
large coloured photograph.

'Our wedding photograph. Look at it. I can't see Dixie
fitting into the Stately Home bit, can you? Not that I
would either, mind — not naturally. But I'm easy and
people accept me, and I sort of fade into the wallpaper.
Dixie's not like that. Dixie doesn't tone in. She sort of
stands out. And she's got a mind of her own. You
wouldn't have met her yet, but you can see it in this snap.
I don't mind who knows it: Dixie's always worn the
trousers in our household.'

'I have in fact had the honour of meeting Lady
Portsea,' murmured Mr Lillywaite. 'I met her briefly
when she arrived at Chetton with . . . er . . . with your
friend.'

'Chokey?'

'That's right,' said Mr Lillywaite, delicately not
mentioning the other occupant of the car, of whom Phil
seemed unaware. 'And in fact I had a long talk with Lady
Portsea only this morning, when she paid a visit to my
office.'

'Dixie did?'

'Yes, indeed. And I may say that Lady Portsea's views
are by no means what you seem to anticipate.'

Phil let out a great laugh.

'Don't tell me, I can guess! Dixie fancies herself in the role of Lady Muck!'

'Lady Portsea, quite naturally, wants what is best for you, for herself, and for the children,' said Mr Lillywaite reprovingly, for though Dixie had inevitably grated on his every sensibility, nevertheless the one thing he really understood was self-interest. 'I would not respect her as I do if she had taken any other view. She was very struck by the case I put before her.'

'That puts a different light on it,' said Phil. 'What Dixie wants, Dixie generally gets.'

Mr Lillywaite had to repress a smile of immense satisfaction.

'I think the best thing,' he said, collecting together his papers, but leaving the book with Phil, 'would be for your wife to pay you a visit.'

'Oh, she's just been. And Dixie was never one for gaol visiting. We're rationed here, you know, same as any ordinary gaol.'

'The Governor is most cooperative,' said Mr Lillywaite, with a little smile of self-congratulation. 'I think you will find there is no problem, and this is certainly a matter that husband and wife ought to discuss together.'

He was in the act of snapping shut the clasp on his briefcase when he happened to gaze down again at the wedding photograph on the table. A group at the Registry Office: Dixie in a shocking pink satin trouser suit of unpleasant shininess, draped in yards of billowing gauze, an expression on her face of great determination and strength of purpose; Phil, by her side, stalwart, mildly embarrassed, complaisant. Really, it could hardly be better.

Suddenly Mr Lillywaite's body stiffened.

'Er . . . who are the charming children?' he asked.

'That's Gareth,' said Lord Portsea, 'and that's little Karen.'

Mr Lillywaite swallowed.

'You mean that at the time of your marriage . . . You mean, to speak plainly, that they are illegitimate?'

'Go on!' said Phil scornfully. 'What a word to use! Nobody worries about that sort of thing these days.'

'I assure you that Garter King of Arms does.'

'Who's he when he's at home? The point is, they're mine. That I do know. I wish I was as sure about the other two.'

'But, Lord Portsea, this is a matter of the gravest importance. Who, then, is your eldest legitimate son?'

Lord Portsea gazed ahead of himself in thought.

'My oldest legitimate son . . . well, that would be . . .' He snapped his fingers and creased his brow, 'That would be — thingummy.'

Mr Lillywaite waited.

'Surely, Lord Portsea, you know the names of your own children?'

' 'Course I do. But this is different. I was married before, see. Wasn't much more than twenty. I was at sea, merchant navy, and I jumped ship in Canada and shacked up with this bird. Bulgarian, she was. Her family got sort of displaced at the end of the war. And we got spliced when she was pregnant. What was his name? . . . Raicho. That's it: Raicho.'

Mr Lillywaite laid his head on the table and wept.

When at last Mr Lillywaite went to have his talk with the Governor he had still not entirely recovered his composure. Nor had he digested the information he had just received. Was this the death-blow to his newly-revived hopes? Or, used properly, could it help him? Lady Portsea had not struck him as essentially the maternal type. Need this weaken her resolve? Were not her ambitions for herself entirely, rather than for herself and her children? In any case, need the full implications be spelled out for her yet? Mr Lillywaite rather thought he saw his way around the difficulties. But what should be done about the next heir?

Meanwhile a glass of sherry in the Governor's flat brought warmth to body, even if it brought no clarity to his thoughts.

'I couldn't be more happy for Phil,' said the Governor, who was the very model of a modern prison governor. The two of them sat on either side of the gas fire, as different as chalk from cheese. 'Splendid chap, didn't you find?'

'Er, yes. Most endearing. I can see he must be popular here. What was his offence?'

The Governor shrugged.

'Nicking goods off a lorry. Pretty much a matter of course in his environment. They don't regard it as stealing, you know. That's why sending him to gaol was so ridiculous.'

'I should have thought,' said Mr Lillywaite acidly, 'that people who do not regard "nicking things from lorries" as stealing need to be sent to gaol to teach them that it is.'

The Governor smiled pityingly. Really, solicitors! What ludicrous survivals most of them were!

'If only we had a proper programme of community work,' he said. 'That's what I would have recommended if I had been asked. Papering some old biddy's room for her . . .'

'Yes. He would be good with old ladies.'

'Restoring some historic building that's been let fall into ruins.'

'I did sense, once or twice, some glimmerings of a sense of the past.'

'Anything like that would be more appropriate. And he

would have been of some use, instead of wasting away behind bars.'

'I got no sense of his having wasted away,' said Mr Lillywaite, sipping his sherry reflectively. 'I wonder a little, you know, about his future . . .'

'Whether he'll go back to crime, you mean? Oh, I shouldn't worry about that. Phil won't nick things if he doesn't have to.'

If there is such a verb as to tetch, Mr Lillywaite tetched.

'*Have to*? I refuse to believe that any able-bodied man is *forced* into crime these days.'

'You misunderstand me. If he were in comfortable circumstances, not demanding too much effort to maintain himself in them, then Phil simply couldn't be bothered to turn back to crime. Too much trouble and too much risk. I think, you know, that for Phil crime was the simplest way of living an easy life.'

'*Not*,' said Mr Lillywaite, 'any great testimonial to his honesty. But still . . .'

'After all, with his coming into this title and so on, he will be rich, won't he? Or at any rate comfortably off?'

'Oh yes,' said Mr Lillywaite. 'If things turn out as I hope, he definitely will be comfortably off.'

CHAPTER 5

THE BLENHEIM WING

Chetton Hall had a long history of birthday celebrations: heirs, in particular, had been celebrated on their comings-of-age with elaborate and protracted festivities involving servants, tenants and estate workers, day-long orgies of home-brewed ale and sirloins of beef, with endless speeches that combined tipsiness and servility in about equal measure. No such marathon jollifications could be put on for the present Earl's sixtieth birthday celebrations: where, for a start, were the servants?

But the festivities did begin early in the morning, and last pretty much throughout the day. Long before Mr Lillywaite had gone to Daintree to interview Phil, the Countess had undertaken what over the years had become a tradition in the Spender family: on this one morning of the year she brought her husband a cup of tea in bed. It was to the Countess's credit that she did not protest at the amount of extra work her gesture involved her in this year. At least, she did not protest to the Earl. She did, under her breath, swear about the height of the cupboards in the kitchen, the fact that the table was yards away from the stove, the ancient nature of the gas stove, which popped alarmingly at the first approach of a match. She muttered, too, at the spectacle of Michele, who drifted into the kitchen in a filmy robe and fetched two glasses of milk from the fridge; but before the Countess could think of anything really cutting to say Michele had drifted out again, looking like nothing so much as an advertisement for dairy produce. When the Countess finally took the two cups of tea on a tray down the long corridors, into the Great Entrance Hall, up the staircase, through the passage behind the Long Gallery and into the State Bedroom, she collapsed beside the Earl in the great bed with a virtuous sense that her part in the festivities was now concluded.

The Earl himself was not idle. He made breakfast, assisted, rather to his surprise, by Dixie. Dixie made several attempts to 'have a word' with him, but always at the crucial moment the frying-pan would spit, or he would have to sprint across the kitchen to the 'fridge for eggs. Soon others began coming in and Dixie's chance was over. Presents began to pile up on the table. The Earl's birthday had not been so lavishly celebrated for years, but, being a modest and an unsuspicious man, he attributed this to his special invitation of them all to Chetton, and felt guilty for putting them all to such expense.

At last everything was ready, and the Earl sent Gareth up with a tray for Granny, and then sat down at table with his own plate to open his presents. He liked them all: the Pagan Passion talc and aftershave that the Countess had picked up in the village store; the box of chocolate liqueurs from Trevor and the warm but tasteful dressing-gown from Joan and Digby, the bandana neckerchief (just a trifle loud) from Dixie and the Kermit soaps from the children; the tin of tobacco that Sam had picked up in Bristol, and the table lighter that Chokey had picked up in a little-frequented room in the Blenheim wing. The children's present touched him most, for he knew how short Dixie kept them. After breakfast all four went to the bathroom with him to watch him wash and shave.

The sun was well up by the time the Countess rose. The Earl had set up a deckchair in the Dutch Garden by the steps to the fountain, and he lay there, snoring lightly, his trousers rolled up and a knotted handkerchief over his head. The Countess, her rather sparse hair gathered into a couple of curlers over each ear, her bulk enveloped in a grubby blue dressing-gown that had seen (and bore evidences from) better days, gazed at him balefully, his evident contentment pricking her hyper-active sense of grievance.

'Doesn't he look a sight?' she said.

Sam, who was in the Dining-Room with her, photographing the Gibbons carvings, merely grinned and went on clicking the shutter.

Not long after this Dixie disappeared. She had made her arrangements with some stealth, by telephone, and then all of a sudden she was marching past her father-in-law down to the fountain where the car was parked.

'Ta-ta,' she called. 'Just going to do some shopping in the village.'

'Best of British,' he said cheerfully, opening one eye. 'There's only four shops. They've got what you want provided you want what they've got.'

But Dixie merely bared her teeth and drove off. Any shopping she did would simply be a cover for the interview she had arranged with Mr Lillywaite. When she returned it was nearly lunch-time, and she bore some brightly coloured cakes from the local baker's. This time she drove round to the courtyard and parked her car by Digby's. Try as she might to hide it, anyone who watched her walk back into the house would have gained the impression that Dixie was as pleased with herself as a cat who has upset the cream jug.

During the morning Lady Joan had cooked a beef stew liberally laced with wine, and they ate in the kitchen. 'Much more cosy,' said Joan brightly. But in fact the kitchen—great, high-ceilinged barn of a place that it was—was far from cosy, unless, perhaps, one had an ox roasting on a spit in the centre of it. The Earls of Ellesmere's consideration for their servants was a matter more of profession than of practical measures. By the late afternoon everyone was gravitating back to above stairs. One advantage of Chetton's vastness was that even on the hottest day a fire was possible, so the Earl lit one in the Green Drawing-Room, and toasted bread for tea. Then with some ceremony he cut the cake that the Countess had made, they all sampled it and the garish buns that Dixie had brought back from Chetton (which did nothing for the reputation of small country bakeries), and eventually, with tea swilling round inside them in great quantities, they all settled down for a typical family get-together.

Like most family get-togethers, this one had its bumpy patches.

'That's nice,' said the Earl, patting his stomach. 'I always said that Elsie's fruit cake was second to none. Did you like it, Karen, love?'

'It was lovely, Grandad.'

'Makes my day, having the children here,' he said, looking around at them all. 'That's what makes it a real family party. Who knows, Joanie: by next year you could have a little addition,'

'You know we're waiting, Dad,' said Joan, rather tight-lipped. 'Till we can really afford it.'

'Well, go to it, Digby,' said the Earl coarsely. 'There's money and to spare from now on.'

Joan cast at him the sort of look she gave to little boys who farted in class. Dixie didn't look too pleased either. Since her talk to Mr Lillywaite she had become a firm convert to the idea of primogeniture, and was preparing to arrange battle-lines accordingly. Still, she could congratulate herself on the four high cards that her brood represented, and was beginning to view with new eyes what she had always regarded as the Earl's fatuous devotion to them. All day Dixie had been quite motherly.

'You shouldn't leave it too long, Joan,' she said, with a tender throb in her voice. 'It's when you're young that you really enjoy children. I tell you, I don't know what I'd have done without them these last few years on my own.'

'I'm not expecting to be without Digby,' said Joan, and added cuttingly: 'especially not *like that*.'

'Now, Joanie, I'm not having that,' said the Countess, cudgels instantly raised in defence of her favourite. 'You're being smug, as per usual. You know as well as I do there's not an ounce of harm in Phil. The worst anyone can say is that he's easily misled.'

'Here, I say—' protested Chokey.

'Naming no names,' concluded the Countess significantly.

'Who okayed the whole plan?' demanded Chokey, his barrow-boy protestations of integrity marred by his gazing at the cornice, the fire-tongs, anywhere but at the Countess. 'Who found out the caff where the drivers always stopped for early breakfast? Who detailed me to get 'em talking and keep 'em there?'

'I said I made no charges,' said the Countess bleakly. 'The fact remains: one gets four years and a record he'll never live down; the other goes scot free. That's not what I call justice.'

'They nabbed Phil when he was just beginning the job,' protested Chokey, his hands fluttering in the agitation of his grievance. 'I hadn't more than passed the time of day with the drivers before the police came and called them out. They couldn't pin anything on me.'

'Seems to me you make a speciality of that,' said the Countess, unmollified.

'Come off it, Mother,' put in the Earl. 'Nobody's blaming you, Chokey, least of all Phil himself. You've been a good pal to Phil, and I know he appreciates you going to see him. I blame myself we haven't been more often.'

'I went when he was in Maidstone,' said Trevor virtuously. Then he spoilt it by adding: 'Just for the giggle. Christ, what a pong in there. Worse than the loo in Piccadilly Underground. Turned me right off.'

'Just you take warning, then,' said the Countess, who was at her most doom-ridden tonight.

'I don't think it's a place to take children,' said Dixie. 'I said to Phil, I said: "You get caught and I'm not bringing the kids to see you." It'd give the little buggers nightmares.'

'It wouldn't,' protested Gareth. 'We wanted to see Dad.'

'Don't you stick your oar in, my lad, or you'll get what-for on your b.t.m.'

'Anyway, no point in poking at old wounds,' said the Earl, beginning to feel uncomfortable. 'He'll be out in three weeks, and I know he won't be bearing any grudges.'

'We could have another party for him,' said Trevor. 'There's this bloke—film producer, actually—that Michele and I would like to get down here. He'd go bananas over this place. He could use it for one of the class-trade films.'

'*Evie and the Merry Monarch*,' said Michele, who only really perked up when her own career was involved. 'Charles the watever-it-was. All those dreamy wigs and ruffles and things.'

'Over my dead body,' said the Countess. 'I'm not having that kind of filth filmed anywhere near me, thank you very much.'

'He'd only need three or four rooms,' said Trevor, 'We could be at the other end of the house, and you wouldn't hear a thing.'

'I'd *imagine*,' said the Countess.

'In three weeks' time we'll be so far away you wouldn't even imagine,' said the Earl optimistically. 'Any party for Phil will be in dear old Clapham. We could get up some kind of street party, like for the Coronation or the Silver Jubilee.'

'I do think, Dad,' said Dixie, speaking carefully, 'that you ought to give Phil a chance to *see* this place. It's silly to make a decision in a hurry, isn't it? When Phil comes out he could come straight here and you could talk it over, face to face. At your leisure, so to speak.'

The Earl frowned.

' 'Ullo, 'ullo, 'ullo,' he said.

'Where did *you* go this morning, Dixie?' asked Trevor.

'Could it be you popped in on old Lillyprick, or whatever the name is?'

'I knew it,' said the Countess, swathed in still deeper gloom, like Cassandra on a bad morning. 'We're not going to be allowed to do what we want with our own. I'm going to be condemned to spend my old age in this rotten dump.'

'That's not it at all, Mum. It would be Phil and me and the kids who stopped here. Look, all I'm suggesting is that you wait till Phil gets out, and talk it over with him. After all, he's the one most concerned.'

'*We're* the ones most concerned,' amended the Countess.

'Not to mention us,' said Trevor.

'I do think,' said Joan, with the infuriating primness she had learned at an evangelically-inclined teachers' college, 'that Dixie's got a cheek. I mean, this is something that only concerns the family.'

'What the bloody hell do you think I am, then?'

'*Not* family,' said Joan, firmly.

'Here, that's enough of that,' said the Earl. 'Let's all have a drink. This is a birthday party.'

And much though some of the family would have enjoyed bringing the thing out into the open, they all looked at each other, swallowed, and trooped towards the bottles. After all, it was his party.

Against all the odds, the rapidly diminishing contents of the old Earl's cocktail bar did wonders for the family party. The present Earl played his part, for he was temperamentally sunny, and a born smoother over of awkwardnesses. Dixie slowly put her claws back in, pleased that she had put the question of Phil's rights on the agenda, if no more. Joan and Trevor, though still in suspense, had been reassured by their father's obvious sense of the fairness of things: they would not, if he had his way, be crushed under the chariot wheels of the elder son's rights.

So before very long things became quite jolly. Clutching their glasses, and talking at the tops of their voices, it became possible to ignore the fact that some were not talking to others. Sam, it was discovered, could play the piano, and play he did—blues numbers first, then some popular songs of the 'thirties.

'*That* brings it all back,' said the Countess when Sam launched into 'Don't Get Around Much Any More', throwing the whole of the upper half of his body into the song, wooing the ill-humour out of his audience. What it was that the tune brought back for the Countess nobody liked to ask (the Earl said it had no particular message for him), but before long she was smiling benignly at the figures of Trevor and Michele, dancing at the far end of the Drawing-Room. And not long after that she was deep in conversation on the green satin sofa with her old antagonist Chokey.

'I well remember,' she reminisced, 'when you and Phil were planning your first job—what was it, seven years ago?'

'Eight,' said Chokey.

'Plans all over the table, stopwatches everywhere, everything timed down to the last second.'

'You never quite recapture the thrill of your first job,' said Chokey, his eyes more watery than ever.

'I thought it was all a big joke,' said the Countess disingenuously.

'Go on.'

'I did. Like boys, planning the raid of the century, all on paper. I never thought you meant to do it.'

'Didn't think we had it in us, eh?' said Chokey, getting up the courage to look her straight in the eye.

'I wish to God you *hadn't* had it in you.'

'Can't keep a good partnership down.'

'Only pity was, you got caught.'

'Yes, well—'

'Seems getting caught was all you ever *were* good at.'

'We weren't always caught. Not on the—not on several of the jobs. Otherwise we wouldn't have stayed in business.'

'Hmmm. What are you doing now?'

'Me? I'm going straight.'

'What are you going straight *at*?'

'Oh, a bit of this and a bit of that.'

Chokey did not mention that one of the bits of this and that had been a house not twenty miles from Chetton, which he and a new partner had tried to relieve of its collection of eighteenth-century china. In any case, the Countess's attention was distracted. Digby and Joan had decorously taken the floor, but Trevor and Michele had got tired of dancing and were slipping out of the far door. The Countess's good mood seemed in danger of evaporating.

'Look at those two. What a trollop that girl is. Where do they think they're going?'

'To get themselves a bite to eat?' hazarded Chokey charitably.

'Ha! I'm not so green as I'm cabbage-looking.'

'Chokey!' came a roar from Dixie. Dixie was never happy for long when other people were getting too much of the action. 'Come and dance.'

Dixie, in her own circle, had only to command. She and Chokey danced smoothly, professionally, beside Digby and Joan's more inhibited performance. Chokey being pear-shaped and Dixie decidedly top-heavy, they fitted very snugly together. The Countess watched them with narrowed eyes. She refused when the Earl asked her to take the floor with him, and went on grimly observing. She hardly brightened when Dixie tired of Chokey and called on Sam to dance with her.

'Man,' said Sam, who seemed to use the word with a nice disregard to sex, 'you tell me the way to dance and play the piano, and I'll dance with you like a shot.'

'There's records in our room,' said Trevor, appearing at the door of the Drawing-Room, somewhat flushed in the face. 'All sorts of old stuff. Seventy-eights and that.'

'Christ,' said Dixie, 'What are they?'

'Come on, man, let's have a look,' said Sam.

So now the party really did begin to go with a swing. Everyone swarmed into the hall, up the staircase, along the Long Gallery, through further corridors to Trevor's suite. Here they were almost at the furthest extent of the old house, where it joined on to the Blenheim Wing. Trevor gleefully began putting on the heavy old records. Even the Countess, heaving her bulk up the stairs well in the wake of the rest, felt her old heart stir again when she heard the strains of long-forgotten tunes; and the children, who had been playing leap-fog in the State Bedroom, felt drawn along too, keeping a weather eye all the while on their mother.

Sam and Dixie danced languorously to 'Slow Boat to China', drifting along the dark, picture-lined corridors. Later they all sang 'Shrimp Boats Is A-Coming' and 'Looking for Henry Lee'. All the older generation seized on the pile of records and shuffled through them with cries of rapture.

'Anne Shelton,' breathed the Earl. 'They don't make singers like her any more.'

'Guy Mitchell,' said Chokey with reverence. 'And Nellie Lutcher.'

'Here—look, Perce. The hokey-kokey! Remember when we did the hokey-kokey on VE night?'

The Countess was rapturous, and jigged experimentally.

'What in God's name is the hokey-kokey?' asked Michele.

'If you haven't danced the hokey-kokey you haven't lived,' laughed the Earl, rubbing his hands with glee. 'Here, Trevor: put on the hokey-kokey and we'll show you how it goes.'

So they put on the hokey-kokey, and the Earl and the Countess demonstrated. Then the children tried it and got the hang of it at once. Then Chokey taught Dixie, and soon the others—who had been watching as if at some aboriginal rite—began tentatively to 'do the hokey-kokey and turn around'. Trevor put the record on again, and again, and they formed a snake, twisting and turning round his bedroom and sitting-room. Then, as the laughter rose to new heights, the snake wound out of his sitting-room and into the corridors. By now the tune was making its own momentum, and soon they were out of earshot of the gramophone, dancing through the corridors and the high-ceilinged rooms of the Blenheim Wing (built by the first Earl with money accumulated when he was Provisioner General to the British Army in France, in which post he displayed a single-minded rapacity equalled only by the great Marlborough himself). Into the marvellous Clock Room they weaved, designed to house the fifth Earl's collection of timepieces; then out the far door, through the Library, almost unused, whose heavy Victorian furnishings failed to dampen their glee. Then finally they hoked and poked upstairs to the top floor, their singing sometimes interrupted by sneezes as the dust got into their noses. Down the dim, small-windowed corridor they went, laughing and singing.

'We could film here,' shouted Trevor to Michele, 'and not a soul would know.'

'Right!' shouted the Earl, who had come to a full stop at the end of the corridor. 'About turn, all!'

'Where's this, Grandad?' asked Karen, gazing at the door.

'Just another room, my darling. We've got more than
enough of those,' shouted the Earl, and began his about-
turn.

But Trevor, his mind full of filming, idly turned the
handle of the door. All of a sudden the dingy corridor
and the revellers were bathed in light.

The door had swung open to reveal a substantial room,
converted to serve as a bed-sittingroom. Heavy curtains
were tacked up close against the windows. By the far wall
two single beds had been pushed together, and opposite
were a table, two chairs, and a small oven. Under the
window were placed a couple of easy chairs. In one of
them sat a portly, putty-faced man, in open-necked shirt
and casual trousers, smoking a cigar. In the other was a
handsome woman, past her first youth, with a confident
manner. The man looked disconcerted, but the woman
looked defiant.

But it was the man who rose to the occasion. Stubbing
out his cigar with dignified meticulousness, he eased
himself out of his chair, advanced to the door, and
inclined his head in the direction of the Earl.

'Was there something Your Lordship required?' he
asked.

CHAPTER 6

THE GREAT HALL

As Joan was later to tell the Chief Superintendent with an
odd pride in her voice, the Earl was like a man trans-
formed. He seemed to be seized suddenly and decisively
by the spirit of his ancestors, a reborn nobleman of the
eighteenth century.

'Well, I'm *damned!*' he bellowed, with that confidence

in dealing with servants that these days can only be displayed by those who have no need of them. 'I can guess who you are. You're the bloody butler or some such flunkey. With your little bit of housemaid floozie in tow. I don't need to ask what you've been doing here.'

The superior squatter, though he had taken a step back in the face of the onslaught, still had some reserves of self-confidence to call on. He said with an attempt at urbanity:

'It seemed to us, My Lord, that there would be no harm in our camping out here, so to speak, until we found our-selves—'

'Oh, that's how it seemed to you, did it? Well, I can tell you, it seemed to you wrong. How would it seem to you if I came and camped in your house, that is when you've stashed away enough of other people's belongings to buy yourself one?'

'Chetton being so large, My Lord—'

'Large or small has nothing to do with it. You just counted on it being so large you wouldn't get caught. Camped out here, my foot! You just tell me when you'll be leaving tomorrow and I'll ring the nearest caravan site: you can take your camping gear along there. Only make it before ten o'clock, because if you're in the house after that I'm going to ring the Meresham police. Got it?'

The man bowed.

'Perfectly, My Lord.'

The Earl banged the door shut, and marched down the corridor, down the stairs, and resumed the long trek back to the Green Drawing-Room, watched and then followed by an unusually admiring family.

Still, the discovery effectively broke up the birthday party. On the way back the children were shooed off to bed. Then the Countess recognized the State Bedroom and trailed into it, saying that all she wanted now was her shut eye. Back in the Drawing-Room the Earl, unusually for him, poured himself a stiff whisky, muttering the while (again, unusually for him) more swear words than had been heard from him over the counter of the ironmonger's in a whole lifetime of service. And though the rest of them poured themselves drinks, the life had well and truly gone out of the jollifications. None of them said so, but they felt, somehow, as if they had become unpleasantly *public* — as if their most intimate actions had been watched and commented on. Only Trevor remained unaffected. But then Trevor was used to having his most intimate actions watched and commented on.

'*Bloody* cheek!' fumed the Earl, incensed rather than calmed by the golden spirit he was downing. 'Hiding themselves away up there. Spying on us the whole time we've been here. Coming out at night, I don't doubt. Do you know, I recognized him? He was down at the Chetton Arms last time we went there. Slipped out as soon as we came in.'

'No one there said anything?' asked Digby.

'Not a word. That's the feudal bloody spirit for you. I've often thought I heard a car in the night, then decided I must be imagining it. You know the smallest little thing wakes me. I bet it's that old Escort that's in the stables. It must be his, or theirs. *Bloody* cheek!'

'I think it's a right old giggle,' said Trevor. 'It really creases me up.'

'It does, does it? Well, it doesn't crease me up. It gives me the gripes. I'd like to know if old Lillywaite knew about this. If I thought he did I'd give him the boot.'

'Dad, he wouldn't,' protested Dixie. 'A man like that . . .'

'He might. After all, I'd told him to pay them off, but he didn't do it very effectively, did he? Perhaps he wanted to keep the tabs on your mum and me. Have somebody here all the time . . . Spying.'

And, in truth, that aspect did seem to make most of the

others a bit uneasy too. After the Earl had downed his Scotch and stumped grumpily off to bed, for all the world like some Hanoverian monarch who has just been defied by his Prime Minister, the others tried to get things going again. Trevor and Michele, whom nothing seemed to affect greatly, intertwined themselves on the sofa, while Digby and Lady Joan had a serious discussion sitting on upright chairs at the far end of the room. Dixie set Sam on to play again, but even though he played 'The Waiter and the Porter and the Upstairs Maid', and Dixie danced desultorily with Chokey, their hearts weren't in it. When both Trevor and Digby had declined to dance with Dixie they began to drift off to bed, some alone, some in pairs. By half past midnight the great house was in darkness.

The first thing to happen on Sunday morning was that a lone figure left the Blenheim Wing and walked (rather jauntily, it must be said) to the stables. A cream Ford Escort was brought round to an unobtrusive door in the wing, and for ten minutes two figures piled it high with possessions as the morning light gathered around them. Then they both slipped nonchalantly into the front seats and the car drove off down the approach road, past the Dower House and the Lodge, and turned right at the gates along the main road to Chetton Lacey. By this time it was nearly seven o'clock, but the house slept on.

The Countess awoke at about eight-thirty. She felt across the width of the great bed, satisfied herself that her husband was preparing her tea, and then drowsed off again.

It was nearly nine when Lady Joan came down to the kitchen. She looked brightly at the mess of glasses left over from the previous evening. She ran water into the sink, squirted a dash of washing-up liquid into it, and then piled the glasses carefully in. She liked to treat nice things properly. Then she put a large saucepan on to boil on the gas cooker, and put some cut bread—how askance she eyed it!—under the grill to toast. Before long Digby came into the kitchen, looking unusually sporty in autumnal open-necked shirt and cream slacks.

'I'm going to boil eggs,' announced Joan. 'It's easier, when you don't know when people will be coming down.'

'Much easier,' agreed Digby. 'I'll put on the kettle and we'll make a big pot of tea.'

They worked in companionable silence, united in a single aim. As Joan popped a couple of eggs into the boiling water, Digby said:

'I slipped down to the stables to have a look. The Escort has gone.'

'Dad will be pleased,' said Joan. 'I must say in this case I see his point. It was an *awful* cheek.'

'Agreed. Anyway, they're out of the way now, but I do think someone should have checked what they took with them. I wish I'd thought to do it myself . . . At least now there's only the family to cope with. I wonder what today will bring.'

'Today will bring Dixie, you can be quite sure of that,' said Joan grimly, lowering her voice to a whisper which echoed round the cavernous expanses of the kitchen.

'That's for sure,' agreed Digby, pouring boiling water into a teapot. 'Still, I think your Dad can cope with Dixie if we back him up. If it were just Dixie, I wouldn't worry. It's this bringing Phil into it that I don't like. If Phil gets the idea—'

'Or gets *given* the idea,' said Lady Joan bitterly. 'He's being put up to it by Dixie and that solicitor, that's obvious. And if the three of them start in on Dad—'

She broke off suddenly as footsteps were heard down the passage. It was Michele, her flimsy nightgown covered this morning by a warm coat, since she had at last realized the refrigerating potential of Chetton Hall. She wafted in, and looked vaguely about her. There was plenty to look at: the kitchen stretched for yards and yards in every direction, and off it opened up various dark rooms, some of considerable size, all of them devoted, no doubt, to some domestic mystery or other in bygone times.

'Hello!' said Joan, all bright and cheery. 'Did you sleep well? Anything you want? I can put a couple of eggs on for you, if you like.'

Michele wafted over to the stove, looked disdainfully at the boiling eggs, then shook her head.

'Just toast,' she said, taking the slices that were under the grill, knifing butter and marmalade on to a plate, pouring two cups of tea, and then drifting out with them all on a tray.

'Little minx,' said Joan, her mouth hard again as she put fresh bread under the grill and turned it up high. 'So inconsiderate. Now the eggs will be overdone.'

Digby and Joan were just decapitating their eggs when Dixie and the children arrived.

'Hello, Digby and Joan! Early birds, aren't you? What worm are you two hoping to catch? Oh — boiled eggs, is it? No, don't stir. I'll do them.' Dixie, resplendent in shining morning face, claret-coloured slacks and frilly blouse, turned to the children. 'Right. Get four glasses of milk from the 'fridge, Karen. Hop to it. Then you lot hook it over there, and don't let me hear a peep.'

Dixie pointed to a distant table tucked into an obscure corner of the great barn of a kitchen — a table where perhaps, in plushier times, the under-tweeny and the rough-work skivvy had eaten their meals apart from the upper servants. The children scuttled there and sat with their milk, watching their elders with round, critical eyes. Dixie, who never understood her children were watching her and taking notes, took five eggs in her large, threatening hands and plopped them into the water.

'Oh, Christ — two of them burst.'

'You only have to prick their ends,' said Joan.

'You watch your language, Joanie,' shrieked Dixie, with a high laugh. She began slapping margarine on bread, while Joan, her little piece of schoolmistressy advice rejected, raised her eyebrows at Digby and spread her toast with lemon marmalade.

'Where the hell are Sam and Chokey?' demanded Dixie, as she took plates of bread and scrape and under-cooked eggs to the children. 'They'll just have to get their own.'

An unnatural quality in Dixie's voice made Joan and Digby glance at each other again: they thought that Dixie knew perfectly well where Sam was, at any rate. They said nothing. Tight-lipped silence was their response to other people's sexual habits. Dixie poured herself tea, and brought cup and plate to the table. She began tucking in, and pretended not to notice the silence around her.

'You know,' she said, supping from her cup thought-fully, 'I've been thinking. It seems to me you two and me ought to get together and have a good talk.'

'Oh?' said Lady Joan.

'About — things,' said Dixie. 'I mean, about here, and all that: the house, and what Dad ought to do with it.'

'Ah,' said Digby, taking charge of the conversation with the silent consent of his wife. Digby was experienced in financial negotiations, and few were the insurance claimants who ever got the better of him. 'Personally I don't see that there's anything much to talk over.'

'Don't be like that, Digby,' protested Dixie, her mouth stretched into an ingratiating smile.

'Well, is there? What are the facts? The options at present under discussion seem to be: one, selling the house and all its contents, with a view to eventually splitting up the proceeds between all the children; two, trying to keep the estate intact for Phil. It's plain as the nose on your face that our interests conflict with your interests. The more Dad tries to compromise and be fair to Joan and Trevor, the less likely it is that the estate could be kept together for Phil.'

'But we could negotiate, surely?'

'You're talking as if Dad had nothing to do with it,' protested Joan. 'We can't negotiate behind his back. It's his decision.'

'Partly,' admitted Dixie, taking a third piece of toast. 'Still, Dad wouldn't want no trouble. Anything for a quiet life, that's your dad's motto. If we three was to get round a table and come to an agreement . . .'

'That's the point I'm making,' said Digby. 'There's no agreement possible. It's one thing or the other, with no middle way.'

'Anyway, it's not only us,' said Joan. 'What about Trevor?'

'Oh, I meant Trevor too,' said Dixie, pushing aside her plate and lighting a cigarette. She smiled at them as if she were a cat playing with two uppity mice. 'Though frankly Trevor doesn't know his arse from his elbow most of the time.'

'Don't you believe it,' said Digby. 'When it comes to the crunch Trevor will know which side his bread is buttered on. People always do. And if he doesn't Michele will tell him. And Trevor's interests are our interests.'

'Anyway, what I'm saying is, if all of us got together—'

'Mum, can we go and play?'

The children had bolted their bread and marge and left their sloppy eggs in their shells, and now they stood around the table in an attitude of hypocritically humble supplication.

'Christ, what did I tell you? . . . . Oh well, yes. Go on, get out. We've got things to discuss.'

The children scampered off to the door, and once they were out of the way Dixie turned back to the discussion.

'I wish you'd try and see my position, though, Digby. And Joan. With Phil . . . out of the way . . . not able to take care of his own interests . . . naturally it all falls to me.'

'It seems to me that Phil is taking care of his own interests perfectly well,' said Digby. 'What with you and this Lillywaite.'

'But he's not here. And you lot are. With a vengeance,' added Dixie, her mask of friendliness dropping for a moment. 'It would be taking advantage if you were to push Dad into making a decision now, without talking to Phil.'

She looked around the kitchen, as if expecting a chorus of assent, but all she saw was the mountainous figure of the Countess, enveloped in her habitual grubby blue dressing-gown, steaming down the passage and into the kitchen with an air of resentment that was almost palpable.

'Here, your dad forgot my tea,' she said. 'It's never happened before in forty years. He must have gone mooning under them trees as usual, and forgot he never brought it up. It's being upset by that butler chappie. Give us a cup, Joanie.'

'Well, fancy Dad,' began Joan, fussing over to the dresser and pouring a cup. 'It's *not* like him—'

But she got no further. She was interrupted by the children, who ran back into the kitchen, their faces screwed up with fear.

'Mum! Mum!'

'God in heaven, you little mongrels, I'll—'

'No, Mum. Come quickly! Grandma! You've got to come! It's—'

'What is it, Karen?' asked Lady Joan, in her practised infants' teacher voice. 'Tell us quietly now—'

'No. Come. Come quickly,' insisted Karen.

First Joan, then Digby, then the rest of them got up and followed the children out of the kitchen. Through the long cold winding passageway they trailed, uncertain and a little apprehensive, then out of the baize door that led down a further oak-lined passage, then finally out into the Great Hall. All of them had crossed the Hall that day—down the stairs and across it, and down those passageways to the kitchen. But none of them had seen what the children pointed to. The Countess looked in that direction, gasped, then screamed.

'Oh, my God! Perce!'

For in the dark little niche made by the stairwell, hunched on his side by the marble by Bernini that Digby had priced on his arrival, lay the body of the Earl. He was in his dressing-gown, and from below it there protruded the bottoms of his pyjamas. His head was tucked into the dark, cobwebby recesses of the wooden panelling, and he was not stirring.

'Oh Dad!' said Joan, going over to him, but stopping some way from him as if he were something a dog had left on a pavement. 'We must get a doctor.'

But no doctor was going to help the Earl now. As Digby strode to the telephone in the Drawing-Room the others stood back, the Countess sobbing, the rest of them staring, at a loss for words. Above their heads, brought there by the scream, could be seen the figures of Sam and Chokey, gazing down on the scene beneath. And everyone there, above and around, knew that the Earl was very, very dead—beyond the help of country doctor or Harley Street specialist. Just as 1936 had been the year in which Britain had three kings, so this seemed destined to be the year in which it had four Earls of Ellesmere.

Four to date, that is.

CHAPTER 7

THE GREEN DRAWING-ROOM

Chetton Hall, with its immensely long and varied history, could not in the nature of things have remained innocent of policemen. The fourth Earl, it is true, after his celebrated attack on his wife's lover, had given himself up, with an air of triumphant self-satisfaction, to a brother magistrate, so the Bow Street Runners had not been needed. But later on, after Sir Robert Peel had established his splendid force, there had been visits from the police, and visits above stairs at that: there had been the involvement of the Hon. Frederick Spender in the Gladwyn Street scandal of 1891, when he was only saved from public prosecution by his threats to implicate the elder son of the Prince of Wales; there was the unfortunate way the seventh Earl's name was drawn into the Tranby Croft affair, and the matter of the wife of the eighth Earl's curious financial involvement with a fraudulent medium. But in all these matters the police had approached Chetton delicately, even hesitantly: would you be so kind, they had seemed to be saying, to subscribe for the moment to the polite fiction that all are equal before the law? No heroine of musical comedy was ever wooed with more tremulous earnestness than was Chetton on these occasions.

This time it was more like a gang rape.

First came a small advance contingent of the law; then came a gang of specialists; then arrived a whole army of supernumeraries. Why so many had been thought necessary by the Chief Constable was not clear: perhaps he thought that Chetton was still swarming with servants and hangers-on, as in the palmy days; perhaps he merely remembered its size. When Chief Superintendent Hickory stomped heavily into the house he quickly sized up the position, and told Sergeant Medway to place this Gilbert and Sullivan chorus of policemen at vital positions around the house and grounds, until the nature and size of the problem could be established.

So Chetton swarmed with policemen. The technical men, of course, centred themselves on and around the Great Entrance Hall: they photographed, observed, took tests. They were men who could reduce the whole complex series of data they noted down about the body and its environs to a neat computer entry—and no doubt before long they would do so. Their voices pentrated distressingly to the Green Drawing-Room, where the family members who had found the body were congregated. Two of the great army of policemen were also there, one at the door to the Hall, one at the door to the Dining-Room. One by one, orchestrated by Sergeant Medway, the rest took up positions: one at the head of Sir Philip's Staircase—a dark, looming man whose eyes went down the magnificent dark carved stairwell, but also along the expanses of the Long Gallery; there was one covering the Main Entrance and courtyard, another in the Dutch Garden; and along the corridors, past the bedrooms, and dotted strategically around the Blenheim Wing there were more and more. It was as if the sheikhs (whom the Earl had not so long ago foreseen as the eventual owners of Chetton) had descended on the place for an OPEC meeting: one would not have been surprised, looking out of the windows, to have seen among the trees and bushes bulky men in dark suits with bulges under their armpits. It was, no doubt, an example of overkill, springing from the fame of the place. But who knew, after all, what a palace of that size might not contain?

Sergeant Medway, for example, was just positioning an extra constable at the junction where the old house joined the Blenheim Wing when a bedroom door opened, and revealed in the doorway was a naked, and very beautiful, Michele.

'Who the bleeding hell are you?' she demanded.

Sergeant Medway was a young man of considerable presence of mind, and he revealed nothing of the warm pleasure that the sight of Michele gave him in the midst of those miles of dreary corridors.

'I'm afraid there's been an accident, Miss. If you'd just put some clothes on I'll escort you d—'

The door banged shut. The Sergeant, raising his eyebrows at his companion, applied his ear to it, but the structural solidity of Chetton defeated him. He, and the constable, waited impatiently.

Downstairs the situation had changed little in the two hours since the body had been found. The Countess was still erupting in watery torrents, dumped ingloriously on the sofa with her daughter perched beside her holding her hand.

'Haven't even got a comfy chair to sit on!' she wailed, as if this were the last straw. 'I never thought I'd lack for that when Perce went. And for him to die just when we was going home!'

Joan, as she seemed to have been doing for hours, said some words of soothing import. She did not have much success. Perhaps the Countess registered their tone, and resented being put on a par with a little boy who has trodden on his favourite Dinky Toy.

The only one to have left the room since the police arrived was Dixie. She had gone over — followed by several pairs of suspicious eyes — to talk to the constable on the door, who had beckoned to another of his ilk, who had escorted her out. Now she and he were in a large, distinguished room overlooking the courtyard, a room that

had served as the old Earl's study. It was a brown,
leathery room of heterogeneous magnificence. There
were fish in cases, photographs of college eights, estate
books and files, and on the shelves novels by Surtees and
Trollope, Desmond Bagley and Dick Francis. On the
square, heavy desk was an array of nib and fountain pens,
and a line of pipes. There was also a telephone.

'I wouldn't want to disturb Mum,' Dixie had explained
to the constable as he led her there. Dixie had long ago
located all the more obvious telephones in the house, and
she was certainly not going to use the one in the Drawing-
Room, with family ears flapping left, right, and centre.
When she realized that the constable escorting her
intended to wait in the open doorway she allowed herself—for she had her broad back to him, and had not
registered the mirror over the fireplace—a fearsome
expression of displeasure. His presence, conceivably,
changed the tone of her conversation. Certainly it
accounted for the fact that, as she spoke, she dotted
convulsively at her eyes.

'But it's *true*, Mr Lillywaite. Found this morning under
the stairs, cold as a—stone cold. I was there myself when
they found him, my own kids it was. It was a *terrible*
shock. We're all shaken to the core, knocked over.
'Specially Mum . . . Yes, she's taken it real hard.
Naturally. They were very close . . . devoted, as you
might say.'

Dixie stopped dabbing at her eyes and put the
handkerchief down on the desk.

'So naturally I feel you ought to be here, Mr Lillywaite.
To deal with the police, and that . . . Oh yes, they are.
Very much so . . . I couldn't say . . . Oh, and Mr Lilly-
waite, I was wondering about Phil.'

Dixie paused, and listened hard.

'But I've heard, from people who know, that they can
be a bit flexible about release dates. And you do see my

point, that he's needed here . . . Well, he is the heir, isn't
he? Everything's his now.'

Dixie was disconcerted by something that sounded like
a dry laugh from the other end of the line. Involuntarily
she took up her handkerchief, blotched black with
mascara. Her mouth slightly open, she listened intently,
dabbing furiously at her eyes.

'But I don't get you. It was you who told me about the
will. What are you trying to say?'

Even the policeman by the door heard Mr Lillywaite's
donnish voice as he precisely enunciated:

'What I am trying to convey is that you are ruined.'

Dixie finished her phone call as best she could, and
banged down the receiver. She pursed her lips, glared
stonily at the policeman by the door, then marched out of
the room, along the passage, through the Great Hall (still
dominated by the small, sad, crumpled body, and filled
with police technicians), and then into the Drawing-
Room. She was observed by them all, but she ignored
them, even her mother-in-law, still sobbing on the green
sofa. Sam, sitting in a corner, his head in his hands but
his eyes open and observant, was not vouchsafed a look.
Nor was the only person present standing up, Chokey,
who was wandering between the Drawing- and Dining-
Rooms, his hands nervously clasping and unclasping. In
his shiny, ill-fitting brown suit he looked, as he gazed at
the furniture and at the ornaments and trinkets on them,
like a down-at-heel dealer at an auction sale, wondering
whether to make an offer for a job lot. Gradually the
Countess's sobs subsided to a snuffle, then to nothing.
The room was blanketed in silence.

'Oh my God! It's true, then!'

Trevor's voice came from the Hall. A moment later,
accompanied by Sergeant Medway, he and Michele
appeared in the doorway. Trevor, unwittingly, had put

on a black shirt of fine silk, and it highlighted the pallor
on his weak, boyish face. He looked appalled. Michele,
too, in a sheath dress the colour of corn, looked as if
something had smashed through the carapace of her
complacency. But then, both of them had just seen the
body for the first time.

'I didn't believe him,' said Trevor, his voice close to
tears, and nodding in the direction of Sergeant Medway.
'I thought it was a kind of have . . . But there he is . . .'

'I'm sorry, Trevor. We forgot about you,' said Joan.

Trevor sank down on to a chair by the fireplace, and
sat looking straight into the empty grate as if he were
about to throw up. Unnoticed by any of them, Sergeant
Medway dismissed the constable by the door with a nod,
and came and sat down in a dark corner of the room.

'Poor old bugger,' said Trevor. His mother erupted
once more into racking sobs.

'Please be a bit more considerate, Trevor,' said Lady
Joan sharply. 'Just when Mum was quietening down.'

'Well, what am I supposed to do? Say "How
unfortunate" and get on with my tatting? . . . I just
couldn't take it in when they told me . . . and there he
was . . . Poor old Dad . . . He was the only one of us that
was any good.'

'Trevor!' protested Joan, more sharply still.

'Be quiet, Joan,' said the Countess. 'He's right.'

'He wouldn't have hurt a fly, Dad wouldn't,' went on
Trevor, as if for once he was seeing things straight. 'Never
had a mean thought in his life. And we all sit around
thinking what's in it for us.'

'Speak for yourself, Trevor,' said Digby.

'Who did it, then?' said Trevor, looking up, his light,
clear voice cleaving through the wide space. 'Who did
that to him?'

There was shocked silence. Joan said in prim tones:
'Nobody has said anything yet about . . . about

anything being done to him.'

'Haven't they? Is that the policeman's annual outing out there, then? You're not going to tell me he just fell. Over banisters that high?'

'He'd had a skinful,' said Dixie brutally.

'He'd had no more than the rest of us. Less. Drank beer all evening until the end. Dad wasn't a drinker, but he could hold as much as any of us. One stiff whisky wouldn't make him rolling drunk.'

The Countess sobbed away, but the rest of them looked at Trevor as if he had uttered an obscenity during High Mass. He, for his part, seemed to have been shocked out of his habitual light cynicism. He looked back at them, aggressively, inquiringly.

The atmosphere was broken by Sergeant Medway. Suddenly when he got up they all realized he was among them: a fair young man with a fair little bush of a moustache and piercing blue eyes, someone who very easily faded into the background (as the Chief Superintendent had told him to fade, while he was with the family) but who, once noticed, could be seen to be a young man of force. Notebook in hand, he spoke to them gently but briskly.

'I'm sorry to interrupt. The Superintendent will want a list of names — of all of you who were in the house last night.'

His briskness was well-calculated. Even the Countess gulped down a sob and looked at him. He went from person to person, bending his thin height over them, and jotting down details in his notebook. All of them had perceptibly stiffened, and kept very quiet. It was as if this routine request provided final confirmation of a fact they had mentally been resisting. Now their quietness was that of people assessing their position. Even Chokey, not unused to police procedures, put an end to his ambulatory inventory of the room and sat quiet. Sam straightened, but kept his cloudy brown eyes alert to the silent drama before him.

When Segeant Medway had been from one to another, asking his questions in a low, respectful voice, he looked around the room to see that there was no one he had missed, then cleared his throat.

'Thank you very much. I don't need to say how sorry I am to have to break in on you at a time like this. I take it this is all the family and guests? Yes? And were there any servants in the house last night?'

'No, there wasn't,' said the Countess, speaking out for the first time. 'We got rid of . . . Oh my Gawd!'

'By Jove!' said Digby. And they all looked round at each other in a fashion almost friendly.

'That butler!' said Trevor. 'That fat-gutted butler!'

'Butler?' said Sergeant Medway quietly. 'Could you give me his name?'

'Can't remember,' said the Countess. He looked at her in surprise, but she was oblivious. 'I heard it once, but it's gone.'

'We were having a bit of a party,' put in Dixie from the window.

'For Dad's sixtieth,' explained Digby.

'And it developed into a knees-up that spread all over the house. And when we got to—' Dixie waved her hand in the direction of the Blenheim Wing—'that bit over there, we were dancing, you see, around all the rooms and corridors, and we got to the top floor, and we were just going to turn around when someone opened a door.'

'I did,' said Trevor, and added, to Medway's mystification: 'Looking for a place to film.'

'And we found this smarmy type and his bint established there. He'd been butler here, so Dad said, and she'd been maid or cook or something, and they'd parked themselves in one of the far-off bits while they waited for another job. The hide of some people! Anyway, Dad really gave them the rounds of the kitchen.'

'He threw them out, did he?'

'He gave them till morning,' said Digby, standing up self-importantly. 'They sneaked away, but I don't know at what time. Dad said the old Escort in the stables must be theirs, but when I went to look for it this morning, it was gone.'

'You could get their names from the village,' said Joan, to contribute to the general helpfulness. 'Dad said he'd seen the man in the public house there. He thought that all the village knew they'd stayed on at Chetton. *Wouldn't* you think someone would have said something?'

'They're not the only ones,' said Trevor. 'Dad thought that lawyer chap — Lillyvick or whatever he's called — must have known too.'

'I'm sure he didn't,' said Dixie, her tones becoming more refined at the thought of the lawyer. 'He's just not the type.'

'We don't all have your personal acquaintance with him,' said Trevor. 'As far as I can make out, he's one of these old family retainer types. Like a butler. They all stick together, thick as thieves. From what Dad said, we were just intruders to him ... . not family, just dirt. I wouldn't mind betting old Lillyvick knew they were here.'

'I beg your pardon.'

A dark, spare shape like a minatory shadow stood in the doorway. Mr Lillywaite's cavernous face, like carved rock, stared around at the assembled family, startled out of its conventional, well-practised expression of sympathy into revealing something of the distaste he really felt for them.

'Oh, you're the lawyer chappie, are you?' said Trevor, quite unintimidated. 'I was just saying you probably knew they were here.'

'Knew *who* were here?'

'That butler and his tart. Camping out in the wing over there.'

'*Parsloe?*'

'That's it,' said the Countess. 'Knew I'd heard it.'

'You astound me. Parsloe still in the house? Most extraordinary. And reprehensible. I most certainly did not know.'

'Pull the other one,' said Trevor, irrepressible in his new energy. 'Seems everyone in the village knew. How come you didn't?'

Mr Lillywaite looked at him fiercely, like some old-style headmaster in a Giles cartoon.

'I have my office in the village; I do not *live* there. I live near Meresham. I have not seen Parsloe since I gave him notice and paid him off.'

'Dad thought he only came out at night,' said Dixie.

'Like some bloody owl,' said Michele. 'Creepy.'

'This,' said Mr Lillywaite calculatingly, 'puts an entirely new aspect on things. Though I can hardly believe . . . What could be the motive?'

The word sank into their consciousnesses.

'Then Dad was definitely done in, was he?' asked Trevor.

'Murder. How appalling,' said Digby.

'That's what I mean by "done in",' said Trevor. 'Could we all now stop beating about the proverbial?'

'We must not jump our fences,' said Mr Lillywaite, regarding Trevor with almost open dislike. 'Still, as I understand the matter, the police believe—'

'Perhaps it would be better to wait a while, sir, until the medical evidence is clearer,' came the voice of Sergeant Medway. Mr Lillywaite jumped. In his absorption he had forgotten the presence of a policeman in the room. He pulled himself up hurriedly.

'Of course. Quite. Quite right, Sergeant.' He tried to relieve the situation. 'I presume you will report to the

Superintendent this extraordinary news about Parsloe?'

'Naturally I'll be doing that, sir,' said Medway quietly. 'And perhaps you could give me the name of the lady who was with him.'

'Well, I imagine . . . I know nothing of the personal lives of the staff, but . . . there were few female servants. The cleaning was done by women from the village. There were no personal maids since there had been no Countess of Ellesmere for many years . . . er, before the present one.' He bowed to the bulky form on the sofa. 'So I rather think the lady with Parsloe must have been the cook. Nazeby. Elizabeth Nazeby.'

'I'm much obliged to you, sir,' said Sergeant Medway, and he handed his list of names to a constable in the hall, then came back and lingered unobtrusively by the door. Mr Lillywaite had been reminded of the proprieties by his recent words, and had approached the Countess on the sofa in the approved consolatory manner.

'Lady Ellesmere, I can't tell you how shocked I was when I heard what had happened. So sudden. Such a terrible shock for you, to find him there.'

'It was that all right.'

'And to think he enjoyed his title, his estate, for such a short time.'

'He didn't *enjoy* them at all, no more did I. They've been a nightmare and a millstone round our necks. All we ever wanted was to get out and get back home.'

She looked at him in silent accusation.

'I assure you, Lady Ellesmere, that I have acted with the best intentions. Remember that there were enormous responsibilities involved.'

'Still are,' said Digby.

'Yes—er—quite. In a sense.'

'I think,' said Trevor, 'you'd better come clean about the position. All this lot's interested in is the will.'

'You have an interest too,' said Michele. 'Don't do yourself down.'

'Ah — I really think this is hardly the time,' fumed Mr Lillywaite. 'I would wish the new Earl to be present.'

'The new Earl's in jug,' said Michele.

'This does concern all the children,' said Digby judiciously.

'Quite,' said Mr Lillywaite. 'But unequally.'

'Unequally?' said Lady Joan sharply. 'I don't see that. I know Dad made a will months ago — when he nearly got run over in Clapham High Street.'

'Oh yes,' said Mr Lillywaite. 'There was that will.'

'What do you mean? Wasn't it legal?'

'Oh yes. So far as I know.'

'Was there another?' asked Digby.

'I hardly think it seemly,' began Mr Lillywaite, in a badgered tone, 'With the Earl lying dead in the Hall —'

The gods were on his side. Just as he was beginning to get a sense of the family forming itself into a pack, driving him to earth in the approved manner of huntsmen, a constable entered from the Hall.

'The Chief Superintendent's compliments, and he'd be obliged if he could have a talk with Lady Ellesmere.'

Dixie was on her feet a second before the Countess.

CHAPTER 8

THE PINK DAMASK ROOM

Dixie recovered herself in a moment, and attempted to retrieve the situation.

'Sorry, Mum. Silly of me. I expect he means you.'

The Countess, cast down as she was, did not deign to reply, but shuffled out of the room on the arm of the young constable, muttering to herself. 'The hide of it,' were the only words audible to her escort. The incident was not lost on anybody in the room: Mr Lillywaite—regretting, not for the first time, his choice of ally—tut-tutted audibly; Sam cast an ironic look in Dixie's direction as she subsided stormily into her chair; while Trevor put his hand up to his mouth and whispered to Michele:

'No prizes for guessing what's been going through Dixie's mind.'

Dixie was hardly capable of embarrassment, but having given herself away so thoroughly she did keep quiet for a bit. In any case, she had no need to say anything. She knew what the others were so keen to find out.

It was Digby who led the renewed attack.

'I don't want to press the point unduly, sir—' Digby made a habit of calling older men 'sir' when he wanted something out of them—'but naturally Lady Joan and the other members of the family would like to know where they stand.'

Mr Lillywaite sighed. He might have known that the family's foxhunting instincts were too deeply inbred to have been eradicated by an upbringing in Clapham.

'This involves,' pursued Digby, 'getting some rough idea of the late Earl's testamentary dispositions.'

'His what?' asked Trevor.

'The will. What I'm trying to say is, we should be told what's in the will.'

'I said the will was all they were interested in,' said Trevor. But he was beginning to be curious himself.

'The Countess not being present—' began Mr Lilly-waite.

'Mum will know all about it,' said Trevor. 'Dad never scratched his—back without telling Mum.'

'No doubt you're right,' sighed Mr Lillywaite,

beginning reluctantly to concede defeat. 'I think the Countess was present when we discussed it.'

'Go on, tell them,' said Dixie, from her seat by the window. 'If there's going to be a row, we might as well have it now, while Mum's not here.'

'Very well; the position is this: when the late Earl came into the property, some six weeks or so ago, I prepared an emergency will, as a holding measure so to speak, designed to meet just such a contingency as has now—regrettably—arisen. It left token amounts—*generous* token amounts—to the two younger children, an annuity to the Countess, and the rest to the elder son, Philip.'

'And this will was legal—signed, and so on,' asked Lady Joan, in a small, high voice.

'Naturally,' said Mr Lillywaite, at his most austere. 'I would hardly let so long go by without tying it up legally. The Earl and I agreed that this was to be a temporary safety-net, a mere stop-gap measure.'

'Until what?' asked Trevor.

'In my opinion, and surely in the opinion of anyone who knows our levels of death duty, the property should have been transferred to the elder son in the late Earl's lifetime. It is the only way to minimize the duties, and the longer the Earl lived thereafter, the better for the heir. I should say in all honesty that I had not convinced the late Earl of the wisdom of this step, though I had high hopes of doing so.'

'You had no hopes,' said Joan, her voice harsh with disappointment. 'Dad was very fair.'

'If it's not a distasteful question,' said Trevor, who was rapidly recovering some of his old insouciant spirit, 'what sort of sum would you describe as a generous token amount? In figures, I mean.'

'The sum was twenty thousand pounds.'

Trevor whistled.

'Not bad. Could be better, but not bad.'

'You're a fool, Trevor,' snapped Joan. 'It's chickenfeed. It would have been much, much more if the old will had stood.'

'It would have meant the dismemberment of Chetton, and of the whole artistic heritage that goes with it, as well as the end of the place as the family's home,' said Mr Lillywaite severely, and with feeling. Then his cratered face collapsed, and he sighed. 'Not that the question arises now. The subject is purely academic.'

'What do you mean?' asked Trevor.

'As I have already explained to Lady Port—to the new Countess, two lots of death duties, as well as the small amount payable on the death of the old Earl, effectively destroy any possibility of maintaining the heritage in the family. There is no way the money can be found and Chetton held on to. It means the ruin of the Spenders.'

His words fell into silence. Dixie, slumped in her chair by the windows, glowered. The rest of them thought, the ticking of their mental processes running a race with the ticking of the ormolu clock on the mantelpiece. Digby raised an eyebrow at Joan. She was a family member. It was for her to put their thoughts—for had they not discussed it, over and over?—into words.

'But,' said Joan hesitatingly, 'death duties are only a proportion. A percentage.'

'A very high proportion,' said Mr Lillywaite austerely. 'I believe that even in the Scandinavian countries, hotbeds of egalitarianism though they are, the proportion is not nearly so high.'

'But even if you take eighty per cent of what Dad inherited here, and then eighty per cent of that, even then—'

'What Joan means,' said Digby officiously, 'is that, suppose the house, grounds, pictures and so on were sold, there would be an amount left to inherit, even after paying the duties.'

'Oh yes, certainly. When I talk of the ruin of the family I refer to their inability to maintain themselves at Chetton after three and a half centuries.'

Dixie, by the window, pricked up an ear.

'How substantial,' asked Digby, 'would the amount left be?'

'A . . . small . . . fortune,' said Mr Lillywaite cautiously.

'And all, now, going to Phil,' said Trevor.

'You see what I meant about the old will,' said Joan, very tight-lipped. 'Didn't Dixie play her cards well?'

Dixie stood up, hands on hips, much of her old good-humour restored. She looked, in fact, like some old bruiser of a tabby, sated on fish.

'Don't be bleeding daft, Joanie. You heard Mr Lilly-waite. That will was made weeks before we came down here.'

'Nevertheless,' said Digby, 'that means essentially that Phil gets the lot.'

'That's the way the cookie crumbles,' said Dixie, a favourite expression of hers when the cookie crumbled to her advantage. 'And when you think of it, it's quite fair. Remember Phil and I have all those kids to bring up, educate—'

She gazed out to the Dutch Garden, where the children were playing very disconsolately. Perhaps she was about to enlarge on the future she planned for them at Eton and Benenden, but she was forestalled by the telephone. The others looked at each other uncertainly, but Dixie—for the moment at least Mistress of Chetton—marched over and lifted the receiver.'

'Yes, this is Chetton . . . Who am I? Lady Portsea—well, Lady Ellesmere, I suppose I should say . . . Yes, it is quite terrible. Shocking . . . Who is it speaking, please? . . . Oh, the *Daily Grub*. Well—'

But she was cut off in mid-sentence. Mr Lillywaite had

strode over, and in the most commanding manner consistent with politeness had seized the phone. He spoke into it rapidly, with finality.

'Yes, it is true that the Earl of Ellesmere has met with a fatal accident. There is nothing the family wishes to add to this. Should it be necessary to issue a statement at a later date, I, as legal adviser to the family, will communicate it to the press . . . No comment . . . No comment . . .'

He banged down the receiver and looked around the room.

'If I may advise you,' he said, in a voice that was far from advisory, 'I would suggest no member of the family answer this telephone. I'm afraid the newspapers are on to the story. We must expect, and shortly, a state of siege.'

The Countess was crying again, but she was no longer wailing with grief. Her sobs were resigned, almost comfortable.

It must have been her interviewer who had done it. It certainly wasn't her surroundings. The Pink Damask Room was a beautiful creation (another of those designed for the lady of the third Earl by her seducer, James Wyatt, who had his fell way with her while the Earl was away with his regiment, attempting to frustrate the Americans of their foolish whim of independence— though to be fair to James Wyatt, he would certainly have had his way with her even had the Earl been at home). But its delicate pink wall-coverings, its two high pier glasses, were not such as to appeal to the Countess—nor, indeed, to Superintendent Hickory, who had been bewildered by the multiplicity of choice, and settled here only because it was suitable in size and conveniently placed.

All of Superintendent Hickory that the Countess was

aware of at this moment was a monumental paunch. This rotund, tweed-clad stomach—clearly part of an immense, weighty man—protruded over the delicate little table that was between them, and it seemed to the Countess comforting: something solid and stable in a shifting world. The stretch of the elderly tweed suggested that this was something that would expand rather than collapse. She did not look at the Chief Superintendent's face, but his voice was reassuring: a rich, slow, warm voice, like drinking stout. It reminded her of days back in the 'fifties when the family had clustered round the radio listening to *The Archers*. It was like having a sympathetic chat with Tom Forrest.

'No, I didn't wake during the night,' she said, her grief now no more than an occasional strangulated sob. 'I did wake in the morning, though—I remember it was light—and I thought he was getting me my morning cuppa, and I went back off.'

'Always got you an early cup, did he?'

'Always!' the Countess wailed. 'Nobody's ever going to get me a morning cup of tea again!'

'He sounds like a good man.'

'He was. One of the best. Trevor just said he was the only one of us that was any good, and for once he hit the nail on the head. Apart from Phil, of course. . . . Neither of them's got a selfish thought in their head.'

'And before all this—' a fat, heavy hand waved round at the work of James Wyatt—'you'd always lived in Clapham?'

'Hackney, and then Clapham. We'd been very happy there . . . nice neighbours . . . brought up the kids there . . . Kids didn't always turn out as we hoped, but there you are.'

'Kids seldom do in my experience. Best not to expect anything.'

'Phil's a nice boy,' said the Countess forcefully, raising

her eyes from the tweedy paunch to look into his face, as
if he had suggested the contrary. But the face, weather-
beaten and kindly, merely looked at her encouragingly.
'One of the best,' she concluded. 'I only wish he were
here.'

'Tell me: over the years, did you ever expect to come
into the title, these estates. Ever talk about it?'

'Never!' said the Countess emphatically. 'Never crossed
our minds. 'Course, we knew we were related.'

'You knew that? Closely related?'

'Yes, we knew that, but we didn't hardly know anything
about the old Earl — what kids he had, how many grandchildren. Didn't have no contact with him — nor want
any, either.'

'You never read about him in the papers?'

'Not to my recollection. He wasn't one of those
personalities, was he? Like Lord Longford, or Lady Olga
Whatsit who has the column. From what we've heard
down here he kept himself very much to himself. Like us,
really. We're very private people, Trevor excepted.'

'So it all came as a rather splendid surprise, did it?'

'Nasty shock, more like. Bolt from the blue, that's what
it was. Rung up by old Lillywaite, then forced to come
down to this horrible place . . . draughty old barn . . . to
be driven from pillar to post by that death's-head skull of
a man . . .'

'Business matters, I suppose? Decisions to be taken?'

'Oh, he was probably only doing his duty. But there's
ways and ways, and I didn't like his, no more did Perce.
Really got Perce's goat at times. Badgered him.'

'Oh, what about?'

'The will. What we were going to do with this hole. I
hold it against him, and always will, that Perce didn't
have no peaceful death. He should have done — gone
gradual: he was the type. Instead of which, day after day,
it was nothing but that dryasdust old stick going on about

making provisions, securing the property, transferring the estate.'

'I'll have to have a talk to Mr Lillywaite,' said Superintendent Hickory.

Mr Lillywaite walked authoritatively around the Pink Damask Room—or at least with an air of authority. He felt perfectly at home there, as he did in any home with pretensions to stateliness, appreciating them not aesthetically, but with a nose for money and tradition. But today he felt less than his usual totally confident self—perhaps because he had recently been checked, by implication rebuked, by a being as lowly as a police sergeant. So he did not look the Superintendent in the eye (as he always did look straight at people when he wanted to impress or bully them). Like the Countess he focused attention on the paunch, and lectured that. The Superintendent, meanwhile, lay back in his chair, as inert as a sack of potatoes, and not much more elegantly covered. When Mr Lillywaite had finished, he asked:

'There had been a previous will, had there?'

'Yes, indeed. Made two months or so previously. It was lodged with some firm in Clapham, and I have no reason to doubt its validity. But of course it was superseded by the present document.'

'I wonder, now, how far the family—'

'Were aware of the document? Quite. Lady Portsea was, as I say. As to the rest: they certainly behave as if they were not. They *did* know about the earlier document, that left the property he had then (such as it was) more or less equally divided. Had the subject come up since they came here? If it hadn't, I doubt if they knew. The Earl and Countess were hardly *writing* people, you know. And it is not the sort of thing most people would want to discuss on the phone.'

'No . . . *Cui bono*,' said the gravelly voice, somewhat

surprisingly, from behind the paunch. 'Most of the usual motives hardly seem to enter the picture here. Hatred, sex, revenge—hardly conceivable, so far as I can gather. Would you agree he was a likeable old boy?'

'Oh—er—' Mr Lillywaite was disconcerted, as always when personal judgements were called for. He was not accustomed to thinking of noble or influential personages in those terms. 'Well, yes . . . I imagine that in his own circles . . . he would be accounted likeable.'

'So that leaves money. Property. Titles. Who profits, and who thought they would profit? Obvious candidates: the new Earl, the new Countess, and their heirs. Call them Phil and Dixie for convenience. Now, I gather the heirs are still children.'

'Ah—hmm. There is perhaps something you should know.'

Mr Lillywaite, whose face had become pained when the Superintendent had so cavalierly put himself on Christian name terms with the new title-holders, once more began to lecture the paunch. His face twisted still further with distaste when he explained the new Earl's family affairs. He was still less happy when, at the end of his disquisition, the Superintendent emitted a fruity, country chuckle.

'Well! This really is turning out to be a beauty of a case! Don't look so dyspeptic, man: this isn't the first titled family with legits and illegits jumbled under one roof. So I take it that the new Lord Portsea was brought up in Canada, and probably knows nothing of his present glory?'

'So far as I know. I don't even *know* that he's alive, though his father seems to assume that he is. If he is, he could be anywhere.'

'Including here. He'll have to be traced. So we can now add a phantom heir to our phantom butler.'

'Ah—so the sergeant has told you.' Mr Lillywaite shook

his head. '*Most* regrettable. Scandalous. I would never have thought it of Parsloe.'

'He was an old family servant?'

'Not quite. The breed hardly exists any longer. You know how it is: these days they come from agencies, with references that *look* perfectly satisfactory. Anyone skilled can demand the earth. Then at the drop of a hat they go off to anyone or anywhere that will pay more — Germany, Saudi Arabia, America. The old Earl's previous butler is, I'm told, now engaged in a similar capacity in the White House. I would have thought he would have had more pride . . . But Parsloe stayed at Chetton for five years, and Nazeby for three. I would have expected better of them.'

'And they were paid off by the late Earl?'

'Yes. A regrettably shoddy business that I warned him against at the time. Not that *that* excuses them . . .'

'You haven't heard that they've got other jobs?'

'No, indeed. My dealings with them were over when I paid them off. They both expressed confidence that they would soon get jobs, and I imagined they had.'

'Hmmm. I suppose there's no way you could know if there was anything missing from the house? . . . No, silly of me. They would hardly take anything obvious.'

Superintendent Hickory rumbled off into a mental by-way, and remained sunk in thought, like some rural sage asked to pronounce on the turnip crop. Mr Lillywaite left him for some time in meditation, then cleared his throat.

'Pardon me. You mentioned motive. Then there is no doubt . . .?'

'Precious little.'

'Might one ask *how?*'

'Karate blow to the neck, then toppled over the banisters, as far as we can see. Medics haven't pronounced finally yet, but that's the gist.'

'A man's crime, it would seem.'

'Not a bit of it. Women take these anti-rapist courses these days. They learn things there that would make your hair curl. Didn't you read in the papers about this poor bloke who fell foul of that pacifist lesbian commune in Leeds? Never be the same again.'

'Dear me.'

The Superintendent relapsed into his brown study.

'They'll all have to stay here,' he said finally. 'Family *and* guests. The thought of interviewing them gives me the willies, but it's got to be done.'

'Come, Superintendent, they may not be quite the thing, but—'

'I'm not talking about their lack of the Emily Post seal of approval. All I mean is that every one of them is going to say he was asleep at the time, and doesn't remember a thing till he woke next morning. And in most cases it'll be true.'

'The crucial time being—?'

'The medics thought early on in the night. Somewhere between midnight and three.'

'So there's no question of the Earl being on his way to make morning tea, or breakfast?'

'None at all . . . You said the new Earl was at Daintree?'

'That's right.'

'Knowing the security at that place, there'd be precious little to stop him from getting over here and doing it. And back before they're called with tea and biscuits.'

Mr Lillywaite coughed.

'On that subject, I should perhaps say I have talked with the prison governor. He was inclined to consider sympathetically the possibility of an early release. On compassionate grounds. He has, after all, only a matter of three weeks to serve before the date set by the parole board.'

'Really?' said Hickory. 'Well, perhaps he will be still

more prepared to release him into my custody, or one of my men's.' He got up slowly, with massive rural dignity, and walked to the windows. Down in the courtyard two policemen were turning very firmly away three battered old cars. 'Reporters. This is going to be the murder of the year, do you know that? There's always one, and this is it. I suspect that with the number of police at Chetton, and the number of reporters around it, Phil will be a damned sight better guarded here than he's ever likely to be at Daintree.'

CHAPTER 9

THE BEDROOMS

'And how are things going in there?' Superintendent Hickory demanded of Peter Medway when, in the middle of the afternoon, they had a chance to compare notes. 'I suppose their thoughts are zooming in like homing pigeons on to the subject of "What's in it for me?" '

'Pretty much,' agreed Sergeant Medway. 'The daughter and her husband are rather inhibited by the thoughts of what might be the done thing in the circumstances. The younger boy seemed genuinely upset, but he's getting the idea that he has to look after number one. The material's there for a good family bust-up, but with a policeman at either end of the room they feel a bit inhibited.'

'Well, as I told you before, if you can get them so used to you that they hardly notice you're there, that could change. I gather they all know that the bulk of the loot goes to Phil, after the Chancellor's had his lion's share?'

'Yes. I suspect one or two of them are pinning their hopes on his well-known good-nature—hoping he'll get a bad conscience about it all. But then they'll have Dixie to reckon with.'

'Not to be trifled with?'

'The thought wouldn't occur: hard as nails, brassy and direct. Most favoured gambit: a kick in the solar plexus. The Bruce Lee of family life.'

'Sounds just my type. Now, the question is: how are events going to shape up when Phil arrives? I've talked to the governor of Daintree, pointed out he'll be a good deal safer here than at Daintree — what with the hordes of cops and now hordes of reporters. I've had to direct men from the house to the grounds, by the by: the men from the Press are congregating around the gate, but the odd fly one is straying: climbing fences, and so on. The fourth estate paying its tribute to the first.'

'I'm not surprised they're interested: this is the story with everything.'

'Nothing like it since Lord Lucan,' agreed Hickory. 'Now, I'm going to send you to get the new Earl. You're a young man who knows how to mix with your betters. If you need to stay overnight you can, because I want you to check up on —'

But he was interrupted by one of his army of constables.

'The lawyer chappie's asked to use the telephone, sir. We've got Philips operating the house switchboard. He says he can cobble your phone in on the same line if you like.'

'Perish the thought,' rumbled Hickory, 'that I should eavesdrop on a legal gentleman going about his business.'

He leaned forward and picked up the phone.

Mr Lillywaite gazed around the old Earl's study with something like complacency on his hard-featured face. It was not that he had any affection for the place, or any happy memories, merely that it put him in mind of the

erstwhile *status quo*. When the young constable had shut
the door behind him, and when his footsteps had been
heard receding down the creaking floorboards of the
passage, Mr Lillywaite took up the phone, got a line from
the switchboard, and dialled.

'Sir Geoffrey?' he said, when he had gone through a
layer of flunky. 'Ahhh—Lillywaite here. I suppose you've
heard the news?'

Sir Geoffrey Watton-Payne was Conservative MP for
the neighbouring constituency of Courtwold. The
member for Meresham, in which Chetton Hall was
situated, was also a Conservative, but he was a young
Thatcherite of the genus flashy suit, decaying roué looks
and messy sex-life. He was not Mr Lillywaite's type at all,
and in all his dealings, business and personal, Mr
Lillywaite liked to stick with the known quantity.

When he and Sir Geoffrey had chewed the cud for
some minutes—and what a mouthful of cud there was to
chew—Mr Lillywaite came to the point.

'It occurred to me, Sir Geoffrey, that you might be able
to help me. I know you have the interests of the County at
heart, and I know you love Chetton Hall . . . Quite . . .
Well, you realize of course that with two lots of death
duties there can no longer be any question of Chetton
remaining in the family . . . Yes, indeed, a bitter blow.
Even with all the special circumstances, a bitter, bitter
blow . . . Yes, quite unsuitable, I'm afraid, but nevertheless I did my best for them . . . I have, as you say, given
my life to it, and to the family. To see the house fall into
the hands of . . . just anyone would be the final straw . . .
Quite. Arabs, Americans, anything is possible. That is
why it now seems to me that the best solution—the best of
a bad job, if I may put it that way—would be if the State
were to take it over as a national treasure . . . perhaps
through the National Trust, as you say . . . special grant
for upkeep, and so on. There are, as you know, special

features which make Chetton quite unique, that cannot be denied . . . I wondered whether the most suitable way to air the question, initially, might not be in the form of a question in the House. Say to the Minister for the Arts . . . Splendid . . . Splendid . . . Tuesday, you say? . . . I need hardly say how grateful I am to you, Sir Geoffrey . . .'

When, after some minutes of itemizing this gratitude which it was needless to express (for servility has maintained its hold in the legal profession longer than in most) Mr Lillywaite rang off, he had the self-congratulatory smile on his face of one whose job has been well done.

Superintendent Hickory waited for the click of the other receiver, then laid down his.

'Wheels within wheels,' he said. 'How matters get arranged. You and I, Medway, and fifty million others, are about to become proud owners of this majestic pile. Now, as I was saying, you're to go to Daintree to pick up Phil. Take your time if needs be, because I want you to check up on any alibi he may have.'

'Daintree's not exactly safe, is it, sir?'

'Tight as a sieve. It's only for fairly harmless birds in their last few months. They regularly pop over the walls and down to the pub of a Saturday night. Locals accept it. Governor turns a blind eye.'

'What about the Governor?'

'Degree in sociology and naive beyond belief,' said Hickory gloomily, and he wished Medway God speed.

As he was driven through the parklands of Chetton, Sergeant Medway began to get for the first time a sense of the immensity of the Earls of Ellesmere's heritage. House, gardens, outhouses, stables, parklands successively unrolled themselves before his eyes. Halfway to the gate was the Dower House — a substantial, early-Victorian building with some traces of Regency elegance — then more and more parklands. Around the gates, peppering the stolid West Country policemen with questions, was a motley and growing assortment of dusty, thirsty men and women, and a straggling of others was to be seen along the road towards Chetton Lacey, peering over walls, prospecting for gaps in hedges.

The constable driving him was all for a chat, but Peter Medway sank himself in thought, anticipating his approaching encounter with the new Earl of Ellesmere.

The Governor, when they arrived, seemed disappointed that the Chief Superintendent had not come himself, but he gave Medway a drink, and (on consideration, since there were no servants' quarters he could be sent to) gave one to the constable as well. He settled them down in chairs, and was clearly spoiling for a chat. The Governor, in fact, was already relishing his role in the Ellesmere saga, and was thinking of allotting it a chapter to itself in his memoirs.

'Phil is down with the checking-out people,' he said. 'We have a certain routine—job prospects, unemployment benefits and so on—though frankly most of it seems pretty irrelevant now. If you want me to hurry them up I can give them a tinkle.'

'No, don't do that,' said Peter Medway. 'The prisoners sleep in huts, don't they?'

'Men. I prefer to call them the men. Yes, they do.'

'Well, with your permission I'd like a few words with some of the other men in the Earl's hut.'

'Then hadn't you better stay the night here and leave early in the morning? It's a question of alibi, I suppose. What time did the old boy catch his packet?'

'The doctor estimates,' said Peter Medway stiffly, for he greatly disliked the man's breezy tone, 'somewhere between midnight and three a.m.'

'Well, I can vouch for him for part of that time. He was up here until about half past one.'

'Here?'

'Yes. I have the men up here now and then. Little social get-togethers, you know. I don't have much social life in this job. My wife lef— my wife and I are separated.' (Peter Medway knew this already. So did half the country. His wife had decamped with a newly-released convict, and their collaborated account of the latter's life and crimes was currently being serialized in the *Observer*). 'So it's good for them and good for me. Last night we had a bit of a meal, then we played cards. Phil's always the life and soul of the party on these occasions. We played whist, then poker. Apart from Phil and myself, there was Garry Thomson (remember those marvellous Dufy fakes that had the art people in such a tizzwozz?). And Ian Rudge who organized that big insurance swindle in the Midlands. We had a really good time, and they left about half past one.'

'I see.'

'He couldn't really have got there and back in the time, could he?'

'He only had to get *there*.'

'Oh yes . . . Of course . . . Well, naturally you've got to check up on these things, but when you know Phil as I do, you'll see that it's quite absurd to imagine him killing anybody. Let alone killing his dad. He was speaking fondly of the old boy only last night.'

'I've heard he's very plausible,' said Sergeant Medway.

'Not just plausible. He's one of the best.'

Sergeant Medway looked up into the shining, guileless, unsuspicious face of the Governor of Daintree.

'I think I'll talk to the men in his hut,' he said.

Superintendent Hickory sent a message through to the family that he and his men would conduct a search of the bedrooms, and that they would then be free to go to them, should they wish. Reports from the attendant constables spoke of all being quiet in the Green Drawing-Room. Very quiet. Nobody was saying a word to anyone else.

Superintendent Hickory heaved himself out of his inadequate little chair and proceeded in a stately way through corridors and Great Entrance Hall, and then up the elaborately carved Jacobean staircase, looking like nothing so much as a Victorian butler bearing bad news on a silver tray. Standing duty at the top of the stairwell was now a WPC, and he decided to take her with him. Superintendent Hickory had considerable faith in the younger policemen, which was a good thing, because he had very little in those of middle age, the intake of the 'sixties. He also had considerable sympathy for the young cops, forced to pay attention to all the conflicting calls of left and right, to steer a middle course between those who expected them to act as untrained social workers and those who nursed subconscious wishes that the police should shoot on sight queers, blacks, pinkos, druggies and any member of any other group that happened at the moment to rouse their spleen. The police were caught in a futile ball game, and he liked to train up the young in the older traditions of the Force.

So he and WPC Hillier — he sedate and brooding, she light and quick — went through the bedrooms closest to the stairs. The geography of the house was simple, once you got the hang of it. On the side of the house overlooking the courtyard the Long Gallery stretched for half the length of the Jacobean house. A small servants' passage separated it from the bedrooms, which looked west, overlooking the Dutch Garden and the Countess's Mile. When the Long Gallery ended, there were bedrooms and retiring rooms on both sides of a gloomy, picture-hung corridor. The Earl and Countess's bedroom, the State one, was some yards from the staircase, but it was something of a disappointment. Not in itself, of course, for though it had been last redecorated for Queen Charlotte's visit in the last years of her life, it had a certain immense, musty, cobwebby grandeur (or, if you preferred it, a certain dreadful Germanic heaviness). But when they got down to a closer look, they found little of interest. The dead man and his wife had occupied it for six or seven weeks, but they had left no more mark on it than overnight visitors. One lipstick, one powder compact, one jar of face cream. Toilet bag and hairbrush for the Earl, and a package of Pagan Passion toilet preparations on the immense commode. A minimum of clothes, all nondescript. Wallet with fifteen pounds in it. A letter from their daughter Joan, and one from Phil. These Hickory took for future inspection.

The children's bedrooms, which they came to next, were no more interesting. Toys, colouring books, dirty clothes. Very dirty clothes. Even the nightdresses and pyjamas were dusty. But then, Chetton was a stupendously dusty house.

Dixie's bedroom was four doors down.

'*Not* next door,' commented WPC Hillier. She peered into the bedroom next to the children's and said: 'No reason why she shouldn't have chosen that.'

Dixie's room gave many more signs of occupation. For a start the dressing-table contained a formidable array of bottles, jars, compacts and boxes, and enough deodorants to make a polecat fit for polite company. Whereas the Countess, it seemed, was beyond any preservation order, Dixie was not, however much she might be in need of plastering. They went through her wardrobe, and WPC Hillier pronounced Dixie's clothes 'a bit much'.

'Flouncy,' agreed Hickory. 'Don't know much about these things, but I'd have thought that with her size . . .'

They looked at the bed.

'Only one slept here last night,' pronounced WPC

Hillier. 'Unless it's been remade this morning, and then got back into.' She went over and looked at the pillow. 'On the other hand, I'd be willing to bet there's been two in this bed at some stage.'

'I wouldn't be surprised,' said Hickory. 'The Countess referred to the West Indian as "Dixie's boyfriend", with a great sniff. Still, we aren't here to discuss their morals, which is as well because it might take an awful lot of time.'

Superintendent Hickory sent his assistant back to the stairwell and proceeded heavily—groaning, like the Countess, at the distances involved—to the further reaches of Chetton Hall.

When Sergeant Medway reached Phil's hut, he found his fellow inmates having their supper. They gave him a wry but not unfriendly welcome: it was like old times, they said, being questioned by the fuzz. Inevitably, and probably truthfully, most of them claimed to have been asleep when Phil came in from the Governor's. Medway had to admit it was perfectly reasonable that they should be. He was more sceptical, in fact, of the two men on either side of Phil who claimed to have woken up.

'Came in at twenty minutes to two,' said the embezzler in the bed on his left. 'Caught his toe on the leg of the bed, and was effing and blinding so much he woke me up. He'd had a few.'

'That's right,' said the bigamist on Phil's right. 'I'd been reading, and I'd only just put my light out.'

'I see,' said Peter Medway, his serene, boyish face showing none of the scepticism he felt. 'Did he go straight to bed?'

'Went to the lav. Then we chewed things over for a bit, then he put out his light and went to sleep.'

'What did you talk about?'

'Guv'nor's little card party, what else? Phil—His

Lordship, I should say—he thinks the Guv'nor's a right berk, like we all do. Phil said if he could get him to the poker school he runs at the Queensbury Arms in Stepney, they'd clean him out in thirty minutes flat and have him out on the streets in nothing but his Y-fronts.'

That, at any rate, had the ring of truth—reluctantly Peter Medway had to concede it. He was just beginning to conclude that Everybody's Pal might indeed have a respectable alibi when the embezzler said:

'Look, mate: if it's a question of Phil bumping off his old man, you might just as well forget it. It's not in character.'

'Right,' said the bigamist. 'If you'd met him you'd know he just wasn't the type. Everyone'll say the same about Phil. He's—'

'I know,' said Medway. 'He's one of the best.'

Slowly, ponderously, Superintendent Hickory heaved his rural bulk along to the suburbs of Chetton Hall. On the borders of the old and the newer parts of the house was the bedroom once occupied by the young Earl that Trevor and Michele had commandeered on their first day. Still on guard there was the young policeman to whom Michele had so memorably revealed herself. When Hickory did his search he took the young man in with him.

It was a difficult room to search, since it was not clear what was the property of the young Earl, and what Trevor had brought with him. Once quality would have told them, but not any longer. The records were doubtless the Earl's, but whose were the silk shirts, the brief male underwear (or was it female?), the sex-shop products, the pornography, the joints? The tastes of the two sets of occupants were obvious, and so similar that neither had put a personal stamp on the room. They went through it with a fine-tooth comb, and the young constable's eyes popped out as he examined some of the contents, but they came away with nothing of interest. (The search, however, did yield results some days later, when the constable met his girlfriend on his first day off, but those results are not of interest here.)

Over the border into the Blenheim Wing was the neat, square bedroom where Digby and Joan had made themselves at home. Joan had even gone out and picked herself a pink rose, and placed it in a toothmug on the dressing-table. So sweet! All their clothes—they had brought stacks—were hung neatly in the wardrobe, and their nightclothes were folded away under the pillow. By their beds were paperbacks. Digby was reading Jeffrey Archer; Joan, Mary Stewart. On the cupboard lay the Wandsworth Public Library copy of the magnificent coffee-table book on Chetton that Mr Lillywaite had used as a bait in his talk with Phil. The room was neat, neutral and decorous. All the searchers found of individuality was a notebook: it contained nothing but figures.

There was a larger notebook in Sam's room further down the corridor. Sam's haversack, labelled Sam Barton, had been dropped near the door, and not fully unpacked. Near it was a little pile of dirty clothes. By his bed was a turned-down copy of *Brideshead Revisited*, as well as the notebook and several pencils. There were figures in this book too, but they appeared to be not money but measurements. The bulk of the book consisted of diagrams and sketches: the West Front of Chetton, with approximate lengths and heights, and placement of windows; the Green Drawing-Room, with estimated proportions; a sketch of the Gibbons carvings in the Dining-Room. The sketches were atmospheric, accomplished. Hickory looked at the constable, raised his eyebrows, and popped the book into a plastic bag.

Chokey's bedroom was hard to find. He had told Sergeant Medway where it was, but his description had been far from clear. It turned out to be a small, musty room at the end of the first floor of the Blenheim Wing. Was he wanting to be some way away from the rest? Or was it his way of proclaiming humility? Or perhaps the big rooms gave him agoraphobia. There were no books, few clothes, no notebooks, no signs of personality. The only written material was a letter from Phil, written from Daintree six months before. It seemed of little interest, but Hickory popped it into a plastic bag.

The room occupied by Parsloe and Nazeby was easy to find, but it contained nothing — no signs whatever of their occupancy. At the end, if only then, they proved themselves the perfect self-effacing servants.

Hickory trailed back along the neat, regular corridors of the Blenheim Wing, at long last arriving back at the Jacobean House. I should get mileage on this case, he thought. But though he walked heavily, his eyes were active, going everywhere. Somewhere in this magnificent warren the vital clue must lie. In the dreary inner corridor between two rows of bedrooms, not far from Trevor and Michele's, he paused. Something wrong. Around one of the pictures the wall covering was darker, greener. No, that wasn't it. That happened elsewhere in the house, even in the Long Gallery. Pictures were from time to time rearranged and rehung. He scratched his head. It was something else. The pictures along the corridor were varied: portraits, landscapes, religious *motifs*. But they were all, surely, of the time of the house's heyday: or, as he put it in his mind, they were all 'class' pictures, the real McCoy. This little landscape was pretty clearly of this century: it had a water-tower in the background. And it was a daub, even he could see that. By one of the family's amateur artists, perhaps. Hickory made a mental note, and passed heavily on.

'I wonder if you'd take a look at this, sir.'

WPC Hillier was still at the top of the stairs, but

obviously she had been tempted to prowl around in so far
as she could without deserting her post. From the landing
stretched to the left the Long Gallery, but to the right
there was only a little runt of a corridor leading to the
north side of the house, a matter of a few yards. Two little
rooms of no obvious purpose opened off from it. What
Constable Hillier pointed to in the corridor was a clump
of earth. No particular significance in that, but—

'What I noticed,' she began, 'was—'

'I can see, lovey. The floor around's dusty, but the
earth doesn't seem to be . . . Recent, then . . . There's
been someone here, and not so long ago. Look, those are
your prints, but *here* . . . and *here* . . . there are prints of
other feet, which have got a film of dust over them
already. Get a measurement of them, so far as you can,
will you?'

Hickory straightened up. The short, aborted corridor
took on a new interest for him. Was there anything else
which seemed to have been disturbed? Yes: under a small
portrait of Lord Portsea, later the eighth Earl, aide-de-
camp to the Earl of Lytton, Viceroy of India, stood a
small oak table, and on it was a heavy brass jug, Benares
ware. On this, unlike the rest of the objects in the
corridor, the dust sat very lightly indeed.

Hickory wrinkled his forehead, stood for a moment in
thought, and then made his stately way down Sir Philip's
Staircase.

Sergeant Medway met Phil briefly that evening, after he
had decided to accept the Governor's offer of a bed for
the night. Phil had just come through the pre-release
programme, and he had been friendly but subdued. He
had remarked, though, that he'd asked how to get his
daily whack for attending the House of Lords, and they
hadn't been able to tell him. Peter Medway fixed nine as
a starting time next morning, and he had spent the rest of

the evening listening to the fatuities which were the wisdom the Governor had culled during his recent years in charge of Daintree.

The next day, Monday, it was shaping up to be another warm July day when they all pitched up round the police car. Phil, though, was wearing a collar and tie and dark trousers. He still seemed preoccupied. He and Medway got into the back seat, and the constable drove off, ears a-twitch: what he wouldn't give to be able to sell this conversation to the Sunday papers! Why was it only *Chief* Constables that seemed able to do that? As the car drove through the gates of Daintree, two on-the-ball reporters, standing by their cars and clearly waiting for them, took photographs of the pair in the back seat. In the evening papers of London and Manchester that day was to be seen on the front page a photograph of Peter Medway staring meditatively ahead, with the caption underneath 'Gaol-bird Earl Released.'

Phil sat for some time, silent and thoughtful. His big hands were lifeless in his lap, his face without expression. Eventually he said:

'Can you tell me what happened?'

Peter Medway gave him a short, simplified account. Phil winced, and his face looked troubled and unhappy.

'Poor old Dad. That it should happen to him . . . I didn't do it, you know.'

'No one's accused you.'

'What those two in the hut said about when I got back was right. All right—if I'd had a car—'

'Quite,' said Medway.

' "Home, James, and don't spare the horses: I have a date to murder my old Dad." . . . Oh, skip it. I know you've got to look into every possibility. I'm not complaining.'

'I've registered that it's a pretty tight schedule,' said Medway. 'We can't rule out the unlikely until we've nabbed someone for it, or at least got hold of a more likely prospect.'

'Any sign of a break-in at Chetton?'

'Not that we've discovered. When you've seen the place you'll realize it's not so easy to check for that kind of evidence. And then there's another factor you probably haven't heard about.'

So Peter Medway told Phil about Parsloe and Nazeby, and their hideout in the Blenheim Wing. It was calculated to appeal to Phil's sense of humour, and he showed for the first time that day the perky self that seemed to endear him to so many.

'What a caper!' he said, smiling broadly. ' "If you're going to squat, squat in style" must be their motto.' His face became serious again. 'Still, murder's something different, isn't it? Knocking off a few choice items I could imagine them doing, but why would they murder?' Medway noticed how different Phil's reaction was from the rest of the family's. Phil seemed almost at once to put them on one side as possible culprits. 'Who else was in the house? All the family, I suppose?'

'I think so. Your sister and her husband—'

'Digby Ferguson, rising star of the insurance world, the genius of the small print and the excuse for not paying out. Nice that the family has some respectable members in it.'

'Your brother Trevor and a girl called Michele Bargate.'

'Willowy, silent, hard as nails and not a stitch of underclothing? No, I don't know her. He always goes for the same type. Conservative as they come is our Trevor.'

'Apart from the family there's someone called Sam Barton.'

'Never heard of him. Who's that?'

'He's a West Indian, I think. Arrived with your wife and—'

Phil laughed out loud.

'Boyfriend of Dixie's, eh? Then he'll probably fade out of the picture as soon as I arrive.'

'Not this one, he won't. Everyone's to stay put at Chetton.'

Sergeant Medway looked sidelong at the new Lord Ellesmere. His hands were quite still in his lap, and his face was wreathed in a relishing, ironic smile. Was Phil that paragon of feminist theology, the unpossessive male? Peter Medway reserved judgement.

'And then there's Len Cartwright,' he said, 'who I think you know.'

'I'll say. Good old Chokey. Taught me all I know.'

'Really? What sort of knowledge would that be?'

'Oh, this and that,' said Phil, slanting a genial glance in Medway's direction. 'You won't get me to shop old Chokey.'

'I gather he has a record.'

'Short as your little finger. *And* years ago. That's when he got the nickname. He's as fly as they come, is Chokey. *And* a heart of gold. Visited me in Maidstone, and in Daintree. There's not many have done that, I can tell you. He's the best pal I've got.'

'I get a bit fed up with hearing about crooks with hearts of gold,' said Sergeant Medway.

'Someone been singing my praises, have they?' asked Phil chirpily. 'That fool of a governor, I suppose. That boy should never have been let loose from the East Cheam Polytechnic. His type gives prison a bad name.'

Phil let out a great laugh at his own wit, and would probably have continued with his views on the Governor, but at that moment they were passing through Meresham, and Phil's eye caught a large hoarding outside a newsagent:

MURDERED EARL: Local Tragedy.

'Mind if I get a paper?'

He popped out of the car, and came back with three papers—one class and two populars. He had also bought a chocolate bar and a packet of cigarettes, and for the rest of the journey he chewed, smoked and read the papers avidly. He expressed indignation at the scant and tight-lipped coverage the story received in *The Times* ('Twenty p, and all it gets is five lines!') but the tabloids absorbed him, and beyond a sudden query as to how his mother was taking it all, he kept silent for the rest of the journey.

It was nearly half past ten when they drove towards the gates of Chetton. The road around was now thick with reporters' cars, and as the police car slowed to get through them, cameras were pushed up against the open windows, and ravenous faces with brown-stained teeth and stale breath shouted questions. Phil gazed ahead, in dignified fashion. Then the gates closed behind them, and they began the last lap to Chetton.

'Bloody leeches!' said Phil. 'I'm not sure how I'm going to deal with them . . . Blimey!' The park stretched out before his astonished eyes. 'I knew the place was big, but . . . What's that? That's not Chetton Hall.'

'I think they call it the Dower House.'

'Just suit us.'

And as, finally, the East Front of Chetton came into view and the car neared the courtyard, Phil let out one of the favourite expressions of his late father:

'By Jove!'

The car pulled to a halt.

'Your new home,' said Peter Medway.

'Be it never so humble,' said Phil. 'Cripes! You'd need Stanley to come looking for you if you went missing in there.'

They opened the car doors and got out. Medway turned to look at Phil, curious to see what the real reaction was, underneath all the jokiness. But from the entrance there came tumbling four shapes of various sizes, shouting and laughing and making a great crowing of triumph.

'Daddy! Daddy!'

Phil waved his hand and ran towards them. He pulled Karen up in his arms and kissed her. He ruffled Gareth's hair and began sparring with Cliff. Then he swung the smallest on to his shoulders and began running towards the house. Shouting and laughing, the five of them romped up the steps towards the door, and then passed through it into the shadows. Where, waiting in the gloom, Peter Medway could perceive the cadaverous shape of Mr Lillywaite.

Thus Philip, thirteenth Earl of Ellesmere, entered the home of his ancestors.

CHAPTER 10

THE CLOCK ROOM

The family had gathered in the Green Drawing-Room to greet the new Earl. There was nothing particularly feudal about this, no intention of curtseying, kissing hands or swearing fealty. It was just that, though they were now allowed back into their bedrooms, there was nothing so comforting or inviting about them as to make them desirable for an extended squat. If you went for a walk in the park you encountered cows, or policemen, or both; the conservatory was so little tended that to walk around it was like a trek through the South American jungle; there was apparently a billiard room somewhere, but nobody had been able to find it. All in all, it was better to stick together, however lugubrious the tone of the resulting gathering.

In any case, they all knew that Phil would soon be arriving, and around Phil, in one way or another, their futures revolved. Some of them were almost apprehensive. Even those who had seen him since his trial had done so too briefly to get more than a fleeting impression of how he had taken to incarceration. So, though none of them had forgotten what he was like, none of them were quite sure he was like that *now*.

When they heard Phil and the children, first from a distance, and then marching through the hall, shouting and laughing together, they all of them, unthinking, held their breaths. They heard Phil say 'Shhh' to the children, heard him put the baby down, and then there he was, walking as cool as a cucumber into their green satin arcadia, followed by the lean, dark shape of Mr Lillywaite.

'Hello, all,' said Phil. 'Bit of a bugger this, eh?'

It wasn't at all what he said. It was just the sound of his voice, the warm, friendly tone of it. They all breathed out, in what was a sort of collective sigh of relief.

'Oh, Phil!' said the Countess, and she heaved her dolorous bulk up from the sofa to give him a hug. When he generously responded she burst into tears on his shoulder, and stood there, clasped to him, sobbing luxurious tears of relief at the comfort of his return.

This particular moment in the drama of the heir's return played to a mixed reception from its audience. Dixie clearly felt rather piqued at the Countess's commandeering of Phil, and had to repress the urge to say something cutting. Mr Lillywaite, on the other hand, looked on with something like approval: this was what the situation called for; this was how the scene should be played. His measured approval was not lessened when Phil, having settled his mother, sniffing quietly, back on her sofa, had a reunion with his wife that similarly accorded with precedent.

'Hello, Dixie, old girl,' he said, giving her a peck on the cheek.

Mr Lillywaite nodded. He could hear—granted the difference in name and accent—the echo of innumerable upper-class and stiff-upper-lipped marital reunions.

Then Phil went around the family. He embraced Joan briefly, and shook hands with Digby. He clapped Trevor on the shoulder and embraced Michele (perhaps for the pleasure of it, perhaps because he did not quite know what else to do with her).

There were only two left, standing a little uncertainly outside the family group.

'Hello, Chokey, old mate,' said Phil, with a wide grin at his partner in crime. Chokey forgot his uneasy shiftings from foot to foot and returned Phil's salutation with a watery grin and a poke in the ribs.

'I know you!' Phil said, when he got to Sam. 'They said Sam Somebody was here, but I didn't connect. You used to live down the end of the road at Clapham.'

'Still do,' said Sam, smiling widely. 'Sam Barton.'

'Well!' said Phil, finishing his royal round of greetings and landing up in the centre of the room. 'I should think we could all do with a cuppa. Who'll put the kettle on?'

Sam volunteered, but he was back in a couple of minutes. The police, unexpectedly considerate, had apparently foreseen the need for elevenses: along with Sam there came what the Countess was already calling to herself 'that nice fair-haired Sergeant'. Both of them bore trays, and soon they began handing round cups of tea and a tin of biscuits. Phil said it was just like the first time he was pulled in for questioning, but before long it began to seem like any other jolly family gathering, and somehow it was not at all unnatural that Sergeant Medway should join the group.

'It's lovely having you home again, Phil,' said Joan, putting it with much delicacy, she thought, and making it

sound as if he had just returned from a tour of duty in the
colonies.

'Great to be here. In spite of—well, you know,' said
Phil, very much your average Englishman in his
unwillingness to talk about death. 'Hey, Chokey, this'll
kill you. Know what the Guv'nor said to me when he said
goodbye?'

Joan, her efforts at genteel evasion wasted, gave a little
moue of dissatisfaction, while Mr Lillywaite grimaced as
if his tea were laced with senna.

'He said, "Well, m'boy, it's been a pleasure having you
here. You've been a real credit to the place." Like it was
my last day at the old school.' Phil, his mother, and
Chokey burst into derisive laughter. 'Then he said, "This
is the opening of a new chapter for you, and I know it's
going to be a happy one." As if I'd won the pools, not had
me poor old dad done in. Stupid git. I don't know how
they pick 'em, I really don't.'

Mr Lillywaite was distressed by the turn the conversation was taking. The conventional modes of reunion
past, he found himself listening to the tales of gaolbirds.
It was not something to which he was accustomed, and in
his distaste he overlooked the fact that Phil's opinion of
the Governor of Daintree was identical with his own.

He said: 'Perhaps you'd like to see round the Hall and
its grounds?'

'All in good time, matey,' said Phil. Mr Lillywaite
flinched. 'Haven't got used to all the old faces yet. Hardly
recognize me own kids, they've grown so much—haven't
you, Karen, my little wonder? Hey—this'll kill you.' He
turned back to his family. 'I went through passing out
drill last night—you know, Chokey: where to go, what to
do, how to keep my hands clean, and what have you. And
true as I'm standing here they handed me the address of
the Salvation Army hostel in Whitechapel, "in case of
need", they said. Cheek of working-classes, eh? I said,

"Come off it, mate: I could invite the whole Sally Army down to my place and still have room for half the bleeding Church of England as well."

They all laughed, even Digby and Joan. Things were really loosening up now Phil was back. He did bring the family together. How had they done without him for so long?

'What a collection!' said Superintendent Hickory, as he shoved across the table to Sergeant Medway the assortment of this and that he had picked up in the various bedrooms. 'And I'm not referring to the noble personages in this house, though I might well be.'

Hickory lay slumped in his chair like some depressive ruminant while Medway went through the various items. When he had finished Medway began to return them to his superior, then had second thoughts about one of the items. He took back and read again the letter Phil had written to his friend Chokey from Daintree, a communication as genially slapdash as his own personality.

Well me old cock Im keeping my pekker up and not letting things get me down not that I ever do you know me. They give you a lot of freedom and I have a bit of a hand of cards now and then with the guvornor whose as nice a chap as youd meet outside of Parkhurst and very libberal with it. You said last time you come you hoped I didnt blame you, what a load of tripe Chokey. More like you should blame me whose plan was it? Of course things are going to be just the same when I get out what do you think. Meanwhile take care, see the kids is alright and remember what I told you. Wo'nt be long now so dont get into any trouble, you need me beside you old mate.

Cheerio,
Phil

'Well?' said Hickory, when Medway had re-read it.

'It *seems* to tie in . . .' said Medway dubiously.

'It seems to be the letter of a born muggins—a dupe, a scapegoat. Is that how he struck you?'

'Not precisely. No . . . Still, he certainly stuck up for his "pal" Chokey. No grassing, and all that kind of thing, pretty much as in the letter. But somehow it doesn't quite . . .'

'What about his wife and her boyfriend?'

'Didn't seem to turn a hair.'

'Born dupe, like I said.'

'Not exactly. He'd have been a dupe if he'd been fooled, but he wasn't. He was—what's the word?—'

'Complaisant. Oh well, I don't suppose it makes a great deal of difference. The letter to Mum and Dad was even less revealing, I thought: starts telling them about the daily routine at Daintree, then gets fed up and signs off mid-afternoon.'

Superintendent Hickory sighed noisily and stood up. He looked dusty and a bit sweaty, and he walked heavily round the Pink Damask Room like a bum bailiff camped in the splendours of Becky Sharp's Mayfair mansion.

'What's going on in there?' he asked, jerking a thumb vaguely in the direction of the Drawing-Room.

'Nothing much. They're beginning to accept my being around, which is something. But all they're interested in at the moment is Phil's tales of what it's like in jug. Bit of a comic, our Phil.'

'What's your impression of him, taken as a whole?'

'On the surface, perfectly nice bloke: funny, sharp, life and soul of the party. Underneath—I just don't know. I wonder whether he isn't much tougher than he seems. On the other hand, he may be chief muggins, like you say: one of these blokes who stick to their mates through thick and thin—the Sir Galahad of the East End. He's a

mystery. I'd like to watch him a bit more before I make
up my mind.'

'You'll get time to watch him. I don't see this case being
sewn up before the end of the week. By the way, there
were a couple of things I found on my tour of this stately
pile.'

And he told Sergeant Medway about the oddly-placed
picture in the bedroom corridor, and the oddities he and
Hillier had discovered in the little corridor off the
landing.

'Interesting, sir,' said Peter Medway. 'But only if they
came about during the night. There'd been people going
round the house for a couple of days before the actual
murder.'

'Right. Though why should they go up a runt of a
corridor that leads nowhere? One reason was given me by
Miss Michele (a hard little bitch, by the way). She said
Chokey had been going round ever since he came exam-
ining all the portable property, as if seeing whether it was
worth nicking. And Sam's been showing a pretty close
interest too. So they may have taken in that little corridor
on their travels, though God knows you'd think there were
several acres of more interesting territory.'

'Does it tie in with anything, sir? With their accounts of
what they were doing during the night?'

'Oh my God, what they were doing during the night,'
said Hickory, recalling the tedium of his interviews with
the individual members of the party. 'It was a case of
"Please, Nanny, I was asleep like all good boys and girls."
Except in one case. This Sam Barton says he was awoken
by something about one o'clock. Now that ought to be of
interest, oughtn't it?'

'Of course. Where's his bedroom?'

'That's it. Miles away, towards the far end of the
Blenheim Wing. If the Earl was clocked with the Benares
ware jug at the top of the stairs—though actually the docs

say it was a manual blow—there wouldn't be a chance in hell of his hearing it from there.'

'Whereas if he were sleeping in Milady's chamber—?'

'He could have heard. Mind you, Dixie's room isn't *that* near: you've got to remember the scale of this place. But he could have heard a body falling from the landing to the hall. He swears he was in his own room, though.'

'Any news of the butler and cook?' said Medway, pursuing a thought of his own.

'None: everybody alerted, both to them and the car. Ports and airports especially alerted, but of course by now we're probably shutting the stable door. I suppose you're thinking that if Sam Barton was in his room—'

'That he wasn't so far from where this pair were hiding.'

'Well, actually he was half the length of Whitehall. But that doesn't alter the fact that that precious pair could have been up to something around that part of the house . . .'

Suddenly Hickory jerked himself out of his contemplative lethargy and seized the phone with the speed and accuracy of a lively bird seizing on a worm.

'I've had an idea . . . Headquarters? Hickory here. Look, I want you to get on the phone to the Yard, and ask them for a list of all the reputable domestic agencies—the *class* ones, the ones that fill positions in the residences of the nobs. Nobs English and nobs foreign. Just get the list, and we'll do the rest.'

He put the phone down.

'I should have remembered. That dry stick of a lawyer mentioned these places. Said they came from one, so the chances are they'd go back there to get themselves another place. If another place is what they want, that is. Right, I think we'd better go and have another look at Sam Barton's bedroom.'

*

It was not until the afternoon that Phil and Mr Lillywaite went on their tour of the house and the estate. Dixie had cooked dinner, and Phil had helped her. They had been left alone in the kitchens by common consent, dearly though the others would have liked to hear what was said. Dixie had planned this as her first opportunity to get Phil alone, and had driven into Chetton Lacey earlier in the day to buy up mountains of steak (causing the butcher to speculate whether the good times might not, after all, be returning at the Big House). Phil peeled masses of potatoes, and they had a cosy chat about the future, during which Phil was rather more noncommittal than Dixie would have liked. They found an enormous old saucepan which could cope with chips, and several frying-pans for the steak. Mr Lillywaite was invited to what he insisted on calling luncheon, but he urbanely declined to (as he expressed it) put them to so much trouble. He went to the little hotel in Chetton Lacey, where they were serving fillet steak and French fries.

When he returned, around two o'clock, the new Earl was having a bit of a zizz — but he jumped up when he heard the lawyer's voice, and they began a tour as wide-ranging and unrestricted as it could be with a whole battalion of policemen cluttering up the route. Phil's eye, as they went slowly from room to room, was appreciative. Mr Lillywaite hoped it was appreciative of artistic worth, but he feared it was of cash value. Not that it mattered — *now*, he said to himself. When they had mounted the Great Staircase and were beginning the tour of the upstairs rooms, Phil turned to his guide and said:

'You know this house and I don't. Would you notice if anything was missing — you know, swiped?'

Mr Lillywaite turned a troubled face in his direction.

'I'm afraid not, Lord Ellesmere. I know this floor only very superficially. I was always seen by the Earl in the study, exceptionally in the Drawing-Room. I have no been up here for several years, except for one visit to the Earl in his last illness — a distressful occasion when I was far from observant.'

(Mr Lillywaite, in fact, had been worrying about his position under the new Earl, a young man of casually impertinent manners and tearaway disposition.)

'Oh well,' said Phil, 'I suppose the fuzz is on to it.'

'You are thinking of Parsloe?'

'Is that the butler berk? Yeah. I was thinking that even if the police do nab them, they could have stashed things away pretty effectively by now.'

Mr Lillywaite was silent. He felt, not quite logically, that he bore some share of responsibility for the Parsloe episode. Throughout the rest of the tour of the house he contented himself with pointing out the most remarkable architectural features, the most magnificent of the family possessions. Phil nodded, and seemed to be taking it all in.

When, finally, they proceeded downstairs again, they passed through the little-used Morning Room and out into the Dutch Garden. Here the Earls of Ellesmere could obtain the most magnificent view of their domain, and Mr Lillywaite paused, that Phil might do so. He had prepared a quote from Sacheverell Sitwell's essay on the house, but Phil got in first:

'Phew!' he said.

It did as well, Mr Lillywaite thought. Phil stood there among the dusty flowers and shrubs, clearly impressed, his feet planted firmly on the paving stones: confident, substantial, watchful. He registered (one could hardly fail to) the hefty, middle-aged police constable at the top of the steps leading down to the fountain. Then his eyes strafed the horizon. He seemed to have remarkably efficient long sight.

'I suppose it's mine to the end of that field,' he said,

pointing into the distance. Mr Lillywaite squinted painfully.

'I expect you mean Parson's Field,' he said. 'Yes. The estates stretch considerably further in all other directions, but to the west of Parson's Field there is a strip of land that the Spenders have always failed to acquire. It was the subject of acrimonious litigation in the eighteen-forties with a farmer called Boythorn.' He turned to Phil with an expression on his face that was close to suspicion. 'How did you know?'

'There's a bloke who just must be a reporter in the field beyond,' explained Phil. 'And a rozzer keeping an eye on him from our side of the hedge.'

They walked down the steps and past the fountain where Charles James Fox had tried to wash away the effects of seventy-two hours' continuous drinking. Then they began along the Countess's Walk. Mr Lillywaite had again fallen silent. He was trying to digest the foregoing conversation. Really the Spenders—*these* Spenders—sometimes surprised him. They had a sharpness, a quickness—on *some* subjects—that disconcerted him. Of course, he told himself, it was not *intelligence*. But nevertheless . . . Even that creature the new Earl's wife had it . . . When they came to the end of the walk, Phil once again gazed around him. They were now at one side of Parson's Field, and Phil seemed fascinated by the figure of the reporter, who was taking photographs from beyond the opposite hedge. Surely, thought Mr Lillywaite, he could not be thinking of *talking* to him? He hurriedly turned the conversation to the topic he had all along been intending to bring up.

'This,' he said, in his thin, acid voice, 'was a favourite spot of your late father . . . in his all too brief residence here. I wonder if we might have a brief preliminary discussion of what your situation is, after his sad and sudden death.'

Phil frowned.

'Stow it,' he said. 'The old boy's not buried yet. Let's do the decent and wait till he's cold, eh?'

Mr Lillywaite felt he had been reproved. No other heir, in his experience, had refused to discuss his financial position at the earliest possible opportunity. Gloomily he wheeled round, and they began to walk back towards the great house.

'Not much to be got out of this,' said Superintendent Hickory, surveying Sam Barton's bedroom with the gloom of a farmer for whom all types of weather apparently portend crop disasters.

'Presumably it's a sort of *pied-à-terre*,' agreed Medway, with a rather magnificent French accent. 'The permanent residence is along the way.'

'Though young people do just dump things down where they land up, and live out of haversacks. These days they do.'

'He's been at Chetton four days,' pointed out Medway.

'Granted. And perhaps he's just come along and taken what he needed and gone back to Her Ladyship. What I don't see is why he should lie. To save Her Ladyship's delicate feelings? She seems as brassy as a country pub. Fear of the jealous husband? By your account Phil is the complaisant husband *par excellence* (if you'll pardon the pronunciation). And you notice there's a book by the bed. So let's assume for argument that on the night of the murder he was here—either for part or the whole of the night.'

'Right. And since it's miles from the staircase, he simply could not have heard the Earl fall. So forget the murder—'

'And start thinking about what else he could have heard. There are these two jokers camped in the wing. I rather agree with the late Earl that they had a bloody

nerve. That being so, they could have decided to play
games with the Earl's property. Presumably with some of
the less famous items. That displaced picture is much too
far away, so let's go walkabout and see what rooms there
are in the vicinity here.'

They went out into the corridor and scouted around,
pushing open doors until Hickory gave a grunt of satisfaction.

'What about this?' he called.

The room he had come upon had been remodelled in
William IV's reign by the same architect who had built
the Dower House—a local man who still looked back on
the Bath of the Woods as the epitome of elegance. The
room was high, airy and well-proportioned, and its
purpose was to display the fifth Earl's magnificent
collection of clocks. Around the walls were the more
imposing specimens, while the body of the room held the
smaller items in a series of display cases and on tables.
Here were the lifetime's acquisitions of a chronomaniac:
the Nuremberg watch from the 1530s; the cumbersome
English church clock, dismantled and reassembled, from
around the same date; the gilt clock with porcelain
figures from Caffieri's; the enamel watch by Fazy. On the
brightness of it all the dust lay thick. The old Earl (who
had no intellectual interests to speak of) had regarded his
ancestor's hobby as an incomprehensible eccentricity,
and had not even been particularly willing to show the
collection to the enthusiastic amateurs who on occasion
applied. The room had been forgotten, or at any rate
neglected, until the dust had temporarily been disturbed
by the hokey-kokey party two nights earlier. Here there
were clocks, but no ticking. Time dominated but it stood
still.

'Now,' said Hickory, 'if there was noise from here—'

'Noise made in the course of nicking something—'

'—then Sam Barton could easily have heard it. Let's

have a good look. You go round—gently, now—to the far end, down there. I'll take this side of the arch.'

It was less than five minutes before Medway made an exclamation of discovery. Not ten feet from the archway that divided the room was a table which, even from the most cursory inspection, seemed to have something missing from it. On it there were five clocks, and an irregular-shaped space on which the dust sat thinly and lightly. Something had been removed.

'Splendid!' said Hickory. 'Measure the area and make a rough outline. If we find that clock, we'll know where it came from. I wonder: could there be a catalogue of the collection?'

He lumbered up to a shelf at the far end of the room, and came back with a slim, leather-bound volume.

'Privately printed in Bristol, in eighteen-forty-seven. Ah—*with* some handwritten additions at the back. I'd be willing to bet the collection hasn't been added to since that particular noble collector died. Now—this is going to be a bit of a fag. Would you like—?'

'No,' said Sergeant Medway. 'Why don't you put WPC Hillier on to it. She's bright and very thorough.'

'Good idea. Right, I'll go and send her along.' Superintendent Hickory stood in the corridor and looked along the great, dark expanse that stretched in the direction of the older parts of the house. 'This place gives me the same feeling I get when I go to London with the wife and she decides to "do" Oxford Street,' he said gloomily, and set off at a modest pace, his bulk forcing up squeaks of protest from every other floorboard.

Sergeant Medway completed his measurements of the vacant place on the table, and was just beginning to get his things together when he saw through the window Sam Barton—also carrying a sketch-pad and pencil—approaching across the lawns towards the Blenheim Wing. The architect, Leoni, had been generous of entrances to his massive extension, and Sam's nearest one was through the Music Room at the far end of the ground floor, and up the elegant stairway which Parsloe and Nazeby had used in all their comings and goings. Medway waited in the corridor to intercept him.

'Just the man I want,' he said.

'Come inside, man,' said Sam, and they passed along into his bedroom. Peter Medway sat on the chair, and Sam sat on the bed. There was an expression on Sam's face that the Sergeant did not know how to interpret. It was—almost—quizzical. It puzzled him.

'Now, this noise you heard—when was it?—about one o'clock.'

'*At* one, man. I turned on the light, had a drink of water, and looked at my watch. It was two minutes to one.'

'I see. And the noise itself: what sort of noise was it?'

'That's what I couldn't get at for your boss-man. Like it's difficult to describe, 'specially as I was half asleep. It was heavy. Sort of a thump, you know?'

'Followed by anything?'

Sam considered.

'Could have been footsteps. Very faint, like pretty far away. But I wouldn't swear to them, man.'

'And you didn't think to investigate?'

'No, I did *not*.' Sam's accent and intonation seemed to become more British, and somehow less of an act, as he explained. 'This house is great, but I don't suppose you've slept in it. At night it becomes something out of Hollywood in the 'thirties—spooky noises, creaking boards, curtains billowing—all that stuff. And then, we'd just had a party. If there were people around, it could have been the party continuing. Or just Chokey coming up to bed: he's just seven or eight doors down. No—I went right back off to sleep . . . Man.'

'So this happened here, right here in this room?'

Sam's quizzical expression returned, and his mouth widened into a grin like a concertina.

'Yes, sir. Right here in this room.'

'You see,' Medway began, rather awkwardly, 'we have to make sure where you were because if you were here you could have heard something being stolen, for instance from the clock room over there. Whereas if you were elsewhere . . .'

'Yes?'

'But you have always, since you came to Chetton, slept in this room?'

'Yes, man: just where my haversack came to rest. But you're not going to believe that, are you? You'd like to have me down the other end of that corridor, and right over near the main stairs, isn't that it? Snuggled up beside Dixie is where you think I was.'

'Well, I—'

'Why do you and your boss-man want to make me Dixie's lover, man?'

'Well, er, you hadn't exactly settled down in this room . . . and Dixie is the only unattached woman guest . . . and you did come here with her.'

'Not bad,' said Sam, nodding his head with approval. 'Quick thinking. But the fact is that since I set foot in this place everyone has assumed I'm Dixie's boyfriend. I expect that's what gave you the idea, not those reasons you've just thought up. So just get this clear, man: I was not in Dixie's bedroom on Saturday night; I have never been in Dixie's bedroom—not here at Chetton, nor back at her home in Stepney, nor anywhere. I've never been in Dixie's bed, and I've no ambitions to get there.'

'Then what, if I may ask, are you doing here?'

'I'm a student of architecture,' said Sam.

CHAPTER 11

THE HOUSE OF COMMONS

'The young man,' said Hickory next morning, slamming down the phone, 'was telling nothing but the truth.'

He had phoned through a query about Sam to Scotland Yard the night before, and they had come up with a report that tallied at every point with Sam's description of himself.

'Student of architecture at Kensington Poly. He's been doing some work with a firm of architects that specializes in these neo-Queen Anne buildings in sensitive areas where a square glass tower block would be out of place.'

'Sort of mock-period stuff?'

'That's it. And a very good idea too, if it means fewer of these concrete and glass jobs. They say they're all the rage. So that explains the interest in Chetton. He told his family he'd met up with Dixie when she'd been visiting Haig Street to check up on her in-laws' house. He'd wangled an invitation down here: he'd wanted to see it for a long time, he told them, but it was hardly ever open to the public.'

'Hmmm,' said Sergeant Medway. 'All this really proves is that he's smart enough not to lie about something he knew would be checked up on. It doesn't prove he's not Dixie's boyfriend, for instance.'

'Apparently there's no talk of that, either in Stepney or in Clapham. As far as I can see, he's got a perfectly plausible reason for being here, and everyone jumped to the wrong conclusion. Whether you put this down to the Spenders' views on blacks or the Spenders' views on Dixie I don't quite know. But the situation at the moment is that Sam Barton's connection with the Spenders is a completely casual one. Now—what's come in today?'

He rummaged around on his desk among papers that had been put there that morning, and finally seized on something with a satisfied 'Ahhh'. He clearly found it absorbing, and Sergeant Medway could only wait respectfully.

'Now that *is* something. They've found the agency that Parsloe and Nazeby used. They were sent particulars of a variety of jobs where both butler and cook were required. Last week they telephoned and accepted a job in Ireland. They agreed to take up residence on the second. That's Saturday.'

'Ireland?' said Peter Medway, wrinkling his forehead. 'Why Ireland? It's all slums and peasants, isn't it?'

'Don't show your ignorance, young man,' said Hickory, easing himself back painfully in his chair to see if there were any position in which he could sprawl. 'Where you have slums and peasants you also have nobs. Half the lusher sort of aristocrat has one of his homes in Ireland. Though in fact it wasn't one of those that they took the job with. It was a writer.'

'Good God! A writer with a butler and a cook?'

'Thriller writer, name of Carleton Milnes. Never heard of him? I bet the old Earl read him. Enormously successful. Fast, exciting stuff. He's very right-wing. Says the nation's lost its backbone, so he's gone to live in a tax haven. It's tax free for writers in Ireland, you know.'

'Good heavens! What an odd idea!'

'I believe they claw it all back from the authors by the tax they levy on whisky.'

'What do we do? Alert the Irish police?'

'You don't know much about Ireland, do you, Peter? There's no power on earth can alert the Garda. They're still looking for Shergar, that lot. The best we can do is send a message to Cork, Waterford and a few other places, and hope that something positively shoves itself under their noses. But of course, if this pair are the ones we're after, then Ireland's probably the last place on earth they'll go to.'.

Hickory shuffled through the pile of papers on his desk, glancing at some of the reports, then shoving them to one side.

'Still nothing from Canada on this Raicho character. Not surprising, I suppose. We only telexed yesterday, and he and his mother could have moved fifty times since the last address our Phil had for them. Could have left the country, come to that.'

He placed a paperweight on the little pile of papers he had made, and he was about to settle down to a slow, rural consideration of what his next move would be when his eye was caught by something outside the window.

'Good Lord. Look at that.'

He heaved himself up, and he and Peter Medway went to look. The Pink Damask Room overlooked the court-yard and the overgrown lawns and gardens beyond. Making purposefully towards the lawns, carrying or wheeling scythes, clippers and lawn-mowers, were most of the younger members of the party at Chetton, led by the new Earl of Ellesmere himself.

'A noble working party,' said Hickory, fascinated. 'Anyone would think he'd been in Dartmoor and got into the habit. Do you think this means the family has decided to pull together?'

It didn't mean that at all. In fact, as soon as breakfast was over, Phil had sensed the beginnings of an Atmosphere. All except Sam had wandered back to the Green Drawing-Room, bored and disgruntled. An air, heavy and sticky as a butcher's shop, hung over the room. The Countess was querulous, and Dixie was quarrelsome. And, with all of them there with nothing to do, it could only be a matter of time before one of them — would it be Digby, or would it be Trevor, needled into it by Michele? — started probing him about his intentions. And Phil was by no means ready yet to reveal his intentions.

'Well!' he said, gazing out of the windows at the Dutch Garden. 'I must say the ancestral acres could do with a bit of attention.'

'We paid off the gardeners,' said his mother. 'What was the point? It wasn't as if we was going to keep the place.'

'Bit short-sighted,' said Phil. 'You want the place looking its best if it's going to be sold.'

Cunning Phil. Several of them perked up, and cast looks at their partners. He had not actually said he was selling the place, but he *virtually* had, hadn't he? Selling the place meant oodles of ready money — money waiting to be shared around — provided the weighty obstacle of Dixie were got over first. Phil had always been so open-handed in the past . . .

'Not that I'm criticizing,' Phil resumed. 'Still, it doesn't give a good impression, having the plants all dusty and dying like that. You don't suppose any of the old gardeners are camped out in the potting shed, do you, Ma?'

The Countess giggled. She loved Phil in his jokey mood.

'Oh, go on with you,' she said.

'Then there's those lawns we passed as we drove in yesterday,' went on Phil. 'Out beyond the courtyard place. They looked like a hippie's haircut. There must be tools somewhere.'

'There's nasty little sheds all over the shop,' said the Countess. 'Full of beetles and cockroaches and I don't know what. I know because your Dad did something now and then — till he saw it was too much for one.'

'Not too much for nine or ten, though,' said Phil. 'What about you nippers watering the Dutch Garden, eh?'

'Yippee!' said Cliff.

'Great!' said Gareth.

'And make sure that more goes on the plants than goes on each other—right? You keep them in order, Karen, love. Then the rest of us can set to and do something about the lawns and hedges.'

Trevor looked at his brother with the sort of open-eyed amazement he used when the Social Security people suggested various unpaid activities for the benefit of the community.

'Give over, Phil! We're on holiday, or we *were*. I haven't mowed an effing lawn in my life.'

'Nothing to it, little bruvver,' said Phil. 'You just point the thing forward and go. It's a fine day, or haven't you noticed? Your tan needs a bit of working on, or you'll never get a part in *Evie Goes to Botany Bay*. Come on, Joan, come on, Digby. And you, Chokey. Ma will make us all a cuppa and bring it out for elevenses.'

And such was the charm of Phil's personality that his mother agreed. And such was the strength of his position that the rest of them allowed themselves to be chivvied outside too. Even Trevor, after a few low words from Michele, stirred from his seat under the picture of Sir Rupert Spender to which he bore such a striking resemblance (Trevor was *posing* under it, to be precise, and thinking of various film scenarios in which the resemblance could be put to some use), and then strolled outside and let himself be caught up in the general activity. The children danced on ahead and showed them the sheds and outhouses where the gardening equipment was housed. Around the far end of the Blenheim Wing they found Sam, sketching a detail of a window cornice. He finished the sketch in a couple of strokes and joined the gang. Finally the little battalion filed its way on to the lawns.

It wasn't, admittedly, the whole party. Dixie had said

she had too much to do, but she'd come out later and watch. Chokey had pleaded rheumatics, but said he'd keep an eye on the children. The Countess had one of her little dozes. By mid-morning the kids were hosing and squealing and splashing outside the West Front, while on the other side of the house a real improvement was to be observed in the dishevelled state of the lawns. The men were attacking these, while Joan made peppery little snips at the ornamental hedges around the courtyard, and Michele drifted around in an enormous straw hat, apparently hoping someone would come along and photograph her in soft focus.

They didn't have a lot of time to talk to each other. Michele did come over and chat to Trevor, but it was clear to everyone what that was about: Michele had decided that Trevor was too full of the milk of human kindness, and had taken on herself the role of screwing his courage to the sticking place. In the event, Trevor was the first of them who managed to have a word with Phil. After Michele left him he did a couple of lengths of one of the small lawns with his hand mower, leaning on it more than pushing it, and trying to look like Sebastian Flyte on one of his better days. Then, when Phil passed him just over the hedge, mowing one of the big lawns, and seated high on a motor mower looking rather like a Master of Foxhounds, Trevor shouted to him:

'This'll push the price up, eh, Phil? Nothing like polishing the silver before you take it up Petticoat Lane.'

'I hate seeing things that've been let go,' Phil shouted back, not stopping. And, to do Phil justice, he had always been a great little handyman in the old days, back in the terrace house in Stepney.

Digby was cleverer, and waited for a pause in the action. He conducted his mowing in a very neat and natty fashion, wiping his forehead now and then to show how much it was taking out of him, and even slipping his handkerchief surreptitiously under his armpits. Nobody had ever before been aware of Digby having armpits. But when the Countess appeared in the courtyard with a tray of tea things, Digby made sure he strolled up for refreshments alongside Phil.

'Satisfying work,' he said. 'Joan and I have really fallen for this house.'

'It's a humdinger,' said Phil.

'Pity so few have been able to see it in the past,' said Digby.

'Oh, I expect a lot more will get to see it in the future,' said Phil.

Digby, though his heart bounded with hope, realized in a moment that this was not at all as categoric as he had hoped.

'I suppose you'll be letting us know your intentions in the course of time?'

'Oh, sure.'

'Because Joan's naturally interested.'

'I'll be telling you as soon as it's decent. Like I said to Lillywaite, with Dad not buried it's just not on to talk about it.'

'Oh, quite,' said Digby.

'Not the done thing at all.'

'Oh, absolutely,' said Digby, heartily.

It was not only at Chetton itself that the future of that great monument to how much could be made out of monopolies under the wisest fool in Christendom was canvassed that day. In the early afternoon the subject was raised in the Palace of Westminster, where that Tuesday the Minister for the Arts was filling in at Question Time before the Prime Minister came down to give the House a series of mini-lectures disguised as answers to questions. It was Sir Geoffrey Watton-Payne who, faithful to his promise to Mr Lillywaite, brought up the subject in the private-notice question.

'Is the Minister aware of public disquiet about the fate of Chetton Hall, one of the pearls of Jacobean domestic architecture?'

Yes, the Minister was aware, and shared the Hon. Member's concern.

'Would the Minister suggest to the Chancellor that the solution adopted recently in the case of Teesdale Manor, in which the Exchequer accepted the house and contents in lieu of death duties, and made a special grant to the National Trust to cover the considerable cost of the upkeep, could well be the most appropriate way of ensuring that this architectural treasure did not fall into unsuitable hands?'

Yes, the Minister agreed that the precedent was there for such a step. Of course he could not commit his right honourable friend the Chancellor in any way, but he agreed that in the circumstances this might well prove to be the best means of ensuring that this notable example . . . and so on, and so forth.

It was at this point that the Member for Bullwark South intervened. The Member for Bullwark South was the hammer of the Speaker, and even sensitive members of his own party were inclined to cringe, turn their heads away, or whimper, when his chain-saw tones were heard (as they so often were) asserting the views of 'the working people of this country', roaring coarse abuse at the more shamelessly capitalistic and absentee Tory members, praising the Russians for their enlightened intervention in Afghanistan, or merely shouting slogans after the Speaker had ordered him out of the House. The Member for Bullwark South was, not to put too fine a point on it, a loud-mouthed bully, and he had never yet been known to intervene during questions to the Minister for the Arts, save once, to demand a subsidy for the Finsbury Park Cooperative of Black Handicapped Female Action

Painters. But he intervened now.

'Would the Minister confirm that the same special terms that were offered to the Maynewaring family of Teesdale would also be offered to the present Earl of Ellesmere and his family?'

Now this was a sneaky one. The inheritor of Teesdale Manor had been the chairman of the local Conservative Association, a one-time MP, and Master of Foxhounds. He and his family had been allowed to live on at Teesdale for a peppercorn rent—though of course there was absolutely no connection between who he was and the special consideration shown in his case—none at all. The Minister began to flounder.

'The two cases are very dissimilar . . . The present family are somewhat distant connections of the previous Earls . . .'

'Second cousins!' said Bullwark South, triumphantly. 'Same as the Maynewarings!'

'The conditions of the Teesdale transaction—'

' 'ighly hadvantageous conditions!'

'—were dictated by special conditions—'

'You bet they were!'

'I have no evidence the present Earl wishes to reside at Chetton . . .'

'Why doesn't the Minister admit straight out that this is class justice, and it's because the present Earl is working-class that he's going to get a different deal from local Conservative Chairmen and suchlike.'

'The man's a gaolbird!' shouted an obscure Tory backbencher.

'Double standards!' bellowed Bullwark South, in his element.

The Minister felt that the matter was getting out of hand. There had been fears at the time that the Teesdale decision might have unfortunate consequences. But still: when all was said and done, there was no doubt that the present occupant was the legal Earl, and the legal heir. The Minister was in favour of primogeniture. He had himself inherited his seat from his father.

'In any discussions I have on the future of Chetton, I will see that the wishes of the present Earl are respected,' he said.

The gardening at Chetton went so well it continued into the afternoon. Lunch was some substantial doorstep sandwiches constructed by Dixie, washed down with some bottled ale that Chokey had discovered in the Butler's Pantry. Afterwards they stretched out on the grass for half an hour or so, and then they went at it again. This time Dixie fulfilled her promise, and though she did not join them, she did bring a chair out into the courtyard, and there she sat, like some Russian noblewoman supervising the serfs at harvest time.

The children had drenched the Dutch Garden during the morning, but rather than come round to the lawns and be under their mother's eye, they had taken themselves off to the kitchen gardens, to weed the vegetables. The rest had resumed mowing and snipping, for the lawns and hedges seemed endless once they had started in on them. Sometimes, since Phil seemed such an unexpectedly tough nut to crack, one or other drifted over to talk to his wife. Dixie dealt easily with Michele's advances: they were, after all, two of a kind, and Dixie had the experience and the weight. She was more genial with Trevor, but killingly on her dignity with Lady Joan. She had a friendly chat with Chokey, but after he drifted back into the house she simply sat there, like some complacent Buddha, or vast Tongan monarch surveying her island fiefdom. She began to feel quite drowsy.

So drowsy, in fact, that she failed to notice when the routines of rural labour, the timeless, Constable-esque activities, were interrupted. Her eyes were reduced to slits, and sometimes her head nodded down into her splendid chest. She noticed a police car driving towards the house, but the police were always going backwards and forwards. She paid it no special attention. The slits of her eyes closed. Dixie dozed.

But the car, in fact, never reached the forecourt where Dixie sat. It had stopped near the working party, and a policeman had got out and hailed the figure of the Earl of Ellesmere, who was hacking at tall grass with a scythe towards the far end of the largest lawn. Phil, grimy and sweaty, had ambled over amiably, glad of the break.

If Dixie had been noticing she would have seen the policeman enter into serious conversation with Phil, gesturing towards the car. Then she would have seen Phil walk over, lean through the passenger window, and talk to somebody in the car. Then she would have seen a young man get out of the car, seen Phil give him a hug, and seen the two of them in conversation for some minutes. Then she would have seen Phil look in her direction in some uncertainty, square his shoulders, and begin ushering the newcomer along the path towards her.

As it was, when she opened her eyes Phil and the young man were no more than a few yards away. The boy was about twenty—dark, sallow, lustrous-eyed, with a soft down on his cheeks signifying a premature attempt at sideburns. His clothes were standard casual, but clean, and his wedge heels suggested that he chafed at his short stature. Before Dixie had entirely collected her senses, the two were up to her.

'Oh, Dixie, old girl, I want you to meet Raicho,' said Phil, with a brave front of confidence.

'What-so?' Dixie's forehead was creased, as if a vague bell had been rung.

'Raicho. You know—you've heard of him. Raicho, my son.'

'YOUR SON!'

Dixie's voice warbled from bass to soprano, replete with all the outraged disbelief of Lady Bracknell at her most handbageous. Then Dixie put on one of her scenes.

CHAPTER 12

PARSON'S FIELD

Dixie had risen to her feet, and stood facing them, hands on hips, biceps bulging beneath her pink blouse. As always when she threw a scene, she was oblivious of all else but the cause of her rage, and now she was certainly oblivious of the figure of Peter Medway, standing casually on the steps of the Great Entrance, watching her.

'And what the bleeding hell does he think he's doing here?' she yelled.

'He's my son, old girl,' Phil patiently explained. 'You know: I told you about him years ago.'

'Oh, I knew you had a by-blow somewhere or other. That wasn't my question, was it? I asked what the bleeding hell he's doing here, *now*?'

'Just come to pay a call, haven't you, son?' said Phil, turning to Raicho, his face wreathed in a paternal smile. 'He's in Europe, you know. It's natural he should want to see his dad.'

'Pardon me while I split my sides. Natural he'd want to see his dad? When his dad hasn't clapped eyes on him since he was six months old?' As Dixie ladled on the irony her face became red with passion. Dixie crossed, or Dixie with a grievance, was never a pretty sight, and she reminded Medway of a sergeant-major apoplectic with outrage. 'I'll tell you what he's here for. He's after the loot—like the rest of this shower.' Dixie gestured in the direction of her family and friends, who one by one had straggled over to watch developments, or merely to enjoy the histrionic display, and were now assembled on the edges of the lawn, simply inviting Dixie's wrath.

'Don't be daft, Dixie. How could he have known?'

'Who are you calling daft? How could he have known? He read it in the f— newspapers, same as the whole bleeding country has by now.'

'It was in the newspapers *yesterday*, old girl. Can you really see the news getting over to Canada, him whipping over here and getting down to Chetton the day after?'

' 'Course he could. Christ, Phil: we're not living in the age of the paddle-steamer. He flew. Anyway, you said he was in Europe.'

'He's just come—'

'Don't you believe it. He was in England, saw the papers yesterday, and down he pops to Chetton. For all we know he could have been down here on Saturday night and done in your dad. Get this, Phil: he's after the money.'

'He doesn't know anything about the money, Dixie. He just came to see me.'

'Christ, you're so bleeding soft you'd win the sucker of the year marathon. He's come down wanting his cut! Got the message? Over and out.'

'You want your head reading, Dixie. Anyway, even if he does, he's as much right as anyone else.'

Dixie glared at him in outrage.

'He's *what*? As much right as anyone else? As much as—' Dixie looked around for a child to clutch to her bosom, but her infant phenomena were still occupied far away among the vegetables, so she was baulked of a fine Mrs Crummles-like effect in the pathetic line. 'As much as Gareth and Cliff? As much as Karen and Damon?'

'He's mine, old girl, I'm sure of that. And he's my eldest.'

A nerve seemed to click in Dixie's forehead.

'You'll regret that crack, Phil. You must be out of your mind, or just plain wicked. We're your family. We're the ones you're supposed to provide for, though God knows you haven't done much providing in the last few years. You've been playing it close, Phil—'

'Playing it close, Dixie?'

'Yes, you have. Even with me, and don't think I haven't noticed. But get this straight. You've inherited this pile—it's all yours, what you can keep from the bleeding government. Yours! It's not your ma's—she's had her go. It's not your sister's or your brother's, however much they'd like you to think it should be. And it's certainly not little Johnny-come-lately's here.'

She took a step towards the dark, sallow boy standing by his father. He seemed inclined to take a step backwards, but by an effort of will he stood his ground, and looked her in the face, his large black eyes taking in every detail of that visage, distorted as it was with passion.

'Get this straight, you. We're your father's family—me and my kids. What he's come into is ours, and we're going to get rid of all these leeches here and enjoy it. You've come here to line your pockets, but you'd better think again, sonny boy.'

'I'd never even heard—'

'Put a sock in it. You heard of the gravy train and you came here to jump on it. Well, get this into your pretty head: there's too many on that train already, and you're not joining it. And I tell you one more thing, for your own good: KEEP OUT OF MY SIGHT!'

And she swung round and lumbered up the main steps, past Peter Medway and into the shadow of the Great Hall.

'Dixie's a bit upset,' said Phil.

'That,' said Hickory, 'was a performance and a half.'

He had been alerted by walkie-talkie from the gate

about the arrival of Raicho Spender, and had watched the scene, fascinated, from a window of the Pink Damask Room.

'She certainly held nothing back,' agreed Peter Medway. 'An awful lot seemed to have been bottled up there.'

'Greed, lust for power, jealousy, spite . . . The Lady Macbeth of East London, that's who *that* lady is.'

'Except for the intelligence,' said Medway. 'Without that, I can't see her as the moving power behind the murder.'

'Can't you?'

'She hasn't got a brain in her head. She's so bloody ignorant she probably thinks Marco Polo invented the mint with the hole.'

'You shouldn't confuse ignorance with unintelligence. Oh— I'm not saying she did it, but she has got plenty of intelligence, the sort that shades off into animal cunning. Notice how she got the point about the boy at once: where's he been recently? where was he on Saturday night? She didn't need time to get her ideas organized. Before very long we're going to have to ask him the same questions ourselves . . . What a pity we can't be flies on the walls at the cosy reunion chat of father and son.'

'Well!' said Phil, as the thundercloud began to lift from the courtyard of Chetton, 'you'd better meet the others.' He led Raicho over to the group on the lawn. 'This is your Aunt Joan and Uncle Digby. This is your Uncle Trevor, but since he's only four or five years older than you I should think that just Trev would do. This is Michele. This is Sam, and that there is Chokey. Old friends of the family.'

Raicho went round, silently shaking hands with one after another. His reception was mostly tight-lipped, though Trevor seemed to think it a great giggle, and

carried it off good-humouredly. If Raicho registered that
his reception was less than rapturous, he gave no sign.
Perhaps he had expected nothing else.

'Your grandma's in the house,' said Phil. 'Having a zizz
if I know the old girl. Well, Raicho: fetch your bag and
we'll find you somewhere to kip. This place has got more
bedrooms than the Hilton, though not so many mod.
cons.'

'Are you sure it's all right?' asked Raicho. His accent
was pure Canadian, but his voice was low and unstrident.
He was gazing round at the stupendous pile that was
Chetton, apparently unable to take it all in except in
stages.

' 'Course it's all right. This place has seen worse family
rows in its time than this one, I can tell you. One of the
Victorian Earls shot his son in the shoulder in a quarrel
about gambling debts. Charming lot we spring from.
Anyway, the place is so big you and Dixie never need cross
each other's paths again. Might be a good idea to go in by
the side bit, eh?'

So while the others evaported into the main block, in
little knots, whispering, assessing the situation, and
conspiring, Phil and Raicho fetched his bag from over by
the lawn and made for the Blenheim Wing. The police
contingent in the house had been stepped down, but a
constable watched them as they prospected round, and he
saw that Raicho's dark eyes were wide as saucers as he
took in the immensity and pompous self-assertion of the
place. Finally they settled on a large bedroom not too far
from Sam's and Chokey's, an imposingly gloomy room
once used by the seventh Earl (who had wanted to get as
far away from his wife as possible, and who had dreamed
here of his overmastering passion, which was to harry Mr
Gladstone out of public life). Phil stood by the window,
while Raicho unpacked with the practised skill of the
young who travel light.

'Most of it's just been washed,' he said. 'I'd only recently got back home.'

'See that,' said Phil, when the young man had put his basic travelling wardrobe in place, and had come over to the window; 'it's all ours—' he pointed—'practically to the horizon over there. All ours till the Chancellor of the Exchequer sends in his bill.'

'Who's the Chancellor of the Exchequer?'

'You mean you haven't got a Chancellor over there? Bet you've got the same thing under a different name. He's the money man in the government.'

'Oh yes, we've got one of those.'

'Well, he's got his beady little eyes on this place. Like to stroll around the ancestral acres while they're still ours?'

'Sure I would. But aren't you tired after all that gardening?'

'So-so,' said Phil, and then added: 'Anyway, I don't fancy meeting up with Dixie just at this moment. If I keep out of her way she'll have to come off the boil. Should be nice in the cool.'

So they walked the estate in the early evening sun, to the chagrin of Peter Medway, who had hoped they would settle down in a room by whose door he could station himself. As they walked Raicho told his father about himself.

'Mum married again—but I guess you know that,' he said. 'It was when I was ten. He's an army guy: a bit rough, but we get on OK. I didn't change my name, though. I'm still Spender. Mum had another kid—a girl called Sally. She didn't want to saddle the next one with a Bulgarian name. I used to get ribbed. Anyway Mum herself has practically forgotten the language.'

Phil looked at his son. Short, self-contained, with the beginnings—young as he was—of a sort of toughness which Phil knew he himself had not had at that age. Not ruthlessness exactly, but still, Raicho was the sort of

young man who would get what he wanted. Phil did not
know what his son wanted, but he thought he might suit
his immediate purposes.

'What have you been doing these last few years?' he
asked, as they walked down past the fountain (watched,
had they known it, by Peter Medway, as well as by several
members of the Spender family from the windows of the
house). 'I kept up for a bit, when I sent the payments,
like. But they sort of dropped off, so I lost touch. Wasn't
even sure of your address.'

'Mum never complained about the payments. She was
married by then. I finished school a year ago, and I'm
planning to go to university—to major in computer
sciences. I've taken a year off in between—sort of
sabbatical. I've been working, then travelling since April.
I had six weeks in Bulgaria. Mum had made contact with
some relatives there. Great place, marvellous bathing.
Then I took the ferry to Turkey, then on to Greece. It was
fantastic—another world from Canada.'

And Raicho told Phil about his early years, his mother's
working in a department store to keep them, her
marriage, the moving around from army base to army
base.

'I'm not blaming you,' he said carefully. 'But somehow
I never seem to have had a settled home.'

'Ever thought of trying England?'

'Not till now.'

They were now at the end of the Countess's Mile, and it
was perhaps not a change of subject when Phil stopped
and pointed around him to draw his son's attention to the
rolling acres on all sides.

'It's all ours to right and left, far as the eye can see.
Straight ahead there's bits that aren't ours. According to
old Lillywaite (who's the lawyer chappy, and dry as last
week's bread rolls) there was some sort of legal to-do in
the last century, but we never got our greedy little hands

on it. See those two scruffy types taking photographs? They're reporters, here on account of your grandad's murder that the police told you about. The land they're on isn't ours. Otherwise it's all Spender country. Sounds like a bloody John Wayne film, doesn't it?'

Raicho surveyed the expanse for some time, his eyes hooded, withdrawn. Then he could not resist asking:

'What are you going to do with it?'

Phil smiled secretly. One more asking that question.

'According to old Lillywaite, I haven't got any choice. He's probably right—he must know his onions. Still, I might manage a bit of fun before the Whitehall vultures descend. Whatever happens, I'll keep you informed. And talking of fun—I'm in the mood for a bit of fun now.'

And without warning, like an arrow from a bow, he strode out over Parson's Field in the direction of the reporters. For a moment or two, uncertain, Raicho stood and watched. The two reporters seemed unable to believe their luck. For a second they too stood immobilized, then one of them began frenziedly clicking his shutter while the other leaned across the hedge and voiced pathetic appeals to Phil to come and make a statement for his readers. It was an appeal that Phil showed every sign of responding to. It happened so fast that it was a moment before Raicho noticed that, from the adjoining meadow, the figure of a police constable had suddenly materialized, walking rapidly in the direction of the Earl, apparently convinced that he was going to leap over the hedge and attempt a getaway across country. Had Raicho looked behind him he would have seen Peter Medway running towards them with the same idea in his head.

But when Phil got to the hedge that divided Spender country from land not so blessed, all he did was extend himself over it and shake hands with the two reporters. The police constable stopped in his tracks, and so did Peter Medway. There was, presumably, no law against an earl talking to reporters on his own land. The constable lingered some yards away, his large country ears a-twitch. By the time that Raicho had strolled, somewhat uncertainly, over to them, Phil was on perfectly chummy terms with the two reporters, as was his wont.

'What's it like to come straight out of gaol to this?'

One of the reporters was small and ratty, with uneven teeth and bleary eyes; the other was gaunt and clad in a disreputable raincoat, in spite of the sunshine. Both of them were indulging in an ecstasy of shorthand, flicking over page after page of their pads.

'Well, it's a cut above Maidstone, I can tell you that,' said Phil, whose cockney accent, even to Raicho's unaccustomed ears, seemed miraculously to have thickened, as if he were auditioning for Mr Doolittle. 'Though Daintree was a bit of a preparation. I used to dine now and then in the gracious apartments of the Guv'nor. Landing in the clink rather runs in our family, you know. The fourth Earl did a stretch in Newgate. Nothing serious—slight case of GBH, I believe.'

'What are you going to do with the place?' asked the ratty little representative of the *Daily Grub*.

'Everyone's asking me that. Naturally I'm not making any decisions yet. Not with me poor old dad still on a slab in the police mortuary.'

'But you hope to keep it on?'

'That's up to them bloodsuckers in Whitehall, so far as I can make out. It's a crying scandal if you ask me. Three deaths within three months, and the Chancellor gets his seventy per cent cut every bleeding time. Dracula was never so thirsty. You ask your readers if they think that's fair. This house has been in my family since sixteen-something, and now it's got to go to some Yank millionaire, just because the Chancellor insists on his whack three times over. No—wait a bit: make that "some fat German industrialist". Your readers would hate that even more.'

'Your father was done in, wasn't he?'

'Mind your language, mate. I've got my feelings. The police are treating it as a case of murder.'

'Who do you think done it—did it?'

'Naturally I can't talk about that. It's out of the q. that one of the family could have done it. The police are keeping me fully informed, and I'm leaving it in their hands. They're a competent body of men, as I'm in a position to testify.'

'Do you intend to take your seat in the House of Lords?' asked the cadaverous reporter, who was crime specialist of the *Daily Telegram*.

'You bet. Natch. I've always enjoyed a good show.'

'Which party?'

'Haven't decided yet. I'll give them all the once-over before I make up my mind. Might be a cross-bencher if it's not too uncomfortable.'

'You wouldn't feel . . . out of place there?'

'No, 'course I wouldn't.' Phil got expansive. 'I think I've got a lot to offer their Lordships. Experience most of them don't have. I bet they debate the crime figures regular, and tut their lordly tut, but none of them's ever been in jug. Except one or two of Harold Wilson's pals, perhaps.'

The man from the *Telegram* laughed loudly.

'So you think they ought to welcome you there?'

'Why not? If you mean they'd be too toffee-nosed for me, you're out of date, mate. They're a mixed bunch there, and no mistake. Scouses, cockneys, and all sorts of scum like me. The only title that means anything any longer is Dame, and no one's offered me that.'

'From what you said it sounds as if you think a lot about your family.'

'The kids? Oh yeah, we get on fine.'

'I meant the Spender family.'

'The hancestors, so to speak? Well, naturally. We've

been here a hell of a long time. Not that we've been all that distinguished—not like the Churchills and that lot. Not statesmen and the like. In fact, we've probably robbed the country blind in our time, and given bugger-all in return. Still, when you start thinking about it, here they've been—*we've* been—for centuries: Earls of Ellesmere, Lord Portseas. And then finally it comes to us . . . to me and my son.'

Phil turned to the sallow, good-looking figure at his side.

'This is my eldest, by the by. The new Lord Portsea.'

Quick as a flash the reporters had their cameras out again, the shutters clicking, the spools whirring. Ten, twenty, thirty versions of the new Earl of Ellesmere and his son and heir Lord Portsea, to decorate the breakfast tables of the nation next morning. As they waited for them to finish, Phil, in a dignified, suitable sort of way, looked pleased with himself. And Raicho, very quietly, seemed to be purring.

Back in the Pink Damask Room the Superintendent was on the phone.

'Yes . . . yes . . . That was it: white, pretty ancient model, I believe . . . Yes . . . Both of them? . . . And they've *what*? . . . Oh Lord: it couldn't be better . . . What do we do? We send a man over, that's what we do!'

He put down the phone, and when Sergeant Medway came in a few minutes later to give an account of the Earl and the reporters, he found the weather-beaten old face of his superior wreathed in smiles.

'Did you ever hear me abuse the Garda, my lad? Did you ever hear me suggest that the Irish police were not the most intelligent, conscientious, dedicated body of men and women in the world?'

'You did say—'

'Did I perhaps imply that they couldn't cope with words

of more than one syllable, that logic was forbidden by
their Church under penalty of fifty Hail Marys? Well,
forget what I said.'

'They've got them?'

'They've got them, and they've got the car. And in the
car they've found what they call "A very pretty piece of
paintin' ", a "very fancy clock", as well as various knick-
knacks that may well come from Chetton. This morning I
would never have believed it possible.'

'And where was this, sir?'

'County Waterford, would you believe it? And you're
the one who's going to fetch them.'

CHAPTER 13

BRYCENORTON TOWERS

The newspaper that the late Earl of Ellesmere had read
daily was the *Daily Mirror*. He had ordered it from his
newsagent the day after his demob from the army (rank
of Corporal in charge of Stores) in 1946, and he had never
wavered in his allegiance. When he had come down to
Chetton he had ordered it from the tiny newsagent in
Chetton Lacey, who had rubbed his eyes at this sign that
the times they were a-changing, but who had delivered it
regularly every morning.

Phil had been no more than a toddler in 1946, and had
grown up with the *Mirror*, but when he came down, early
on the Wednesday morning, and flicked through it, he
found it far from satisfactory. True the *Mirror*, like the
rest of Fleet Street, was finding the death of their faithful
subscriber a great source of amusement, what with
Parliament in the last weeks of a dull session and the silly
season just around the corner. But the *Mirror* only had a

picture of the flurry of policemen at the gates of Chetton,
and a fanciful story concocted out of nothing (for Hickory
was not the sort of policeman to babble to the press to
cover over the fact that no substantial progress had been
made). So Phil, skimming through it, just shook his head.

The policeman in the Great Hall did not greatly like
Phil's idea of driving into Chetton Lacey to buy more of
the daily press, but since Sam at that moment put in an
appearance on the stairs, he was sent in the Chetton
estate car to pick up the *Grub* and the *Telegram*, with the
promise of a slap-up breakfast when he returned.

Then Phil trekked off to the kitchens, grilled some
bacon and tomatoes, fried himself an egg, and while he
ate them read through the *Mirror* again. As the others
came down in ones and twos he grilled and fried more
food for them, but when Sam returned with the papers,
he handed him a brimming plate, said 'Here's yours. The
rest can eat bloody muesli,' and retired to the Green
Drawing-Room. Here he settled down on the green sofa
and gave the papers the sort of concentrated attention
that at that hour of the morning is only usually given to
Open University courses. He was not disappointed.

COCKNEY EARL TALKS TO 'GRUB'
'BETTER THAN MAIDSTONE' HE SAYS

The *Grub*'s coverage was sparky and vivid (for the ratty
reporter knew he was competing with those extraordinary
boobs on page 3). It exuded the reporter's sense of being
absolutely chuffed with himself over his scoop, and Phil's
personality emerged as ripe and genial—an impression
supplemented by the picture of him with his arm round
Raicho's shoulder. The *Telegram*'s coverage was soberer,
slightly more grammatical, but it was quite as long, and
used a similar picture. Both papers began their stories on
page 1, and continued them inside. Phil read them both
through twice, then left them conspicuously on the coffee

table by the fireplace.

Down in the kitchen things were sticky. Raicho, hungry enough to brave the dangers of Dixie, had come down in search of breakfast. His dark, good-looking face was apprehensive, but Dixie had luckily kept to her room. The welcome from the others was cold and appraising, but after a second or two's thought Joan said brightly 'Hello, Raicho. I expect you'd like something to eat, wouldn't you?' And she fetched him something with fairly good grace. The rest of them turned back to what they were doing, which was trying to worm information out of Sam.

'But what was he after?' Trevor asked. 'Phil's never been a great newspaper reader before.'

'You ask him, man,' said Sam, who at strategic moments retreated into racial stereotype, even to rolling his eyes. 'He just sent me for some papers.'

'Well, which ones?'

'The *Grub* and the *Telegram*.'

'Why those two? What was in them?'

'He-ell, I dunno, man,' lied Sam. 'I didn't look.'

'I expect it was the interview,' said Raicho. There was a moment's silence. They all turned their eyes to him, suspicious.

'What interview?' demanded Digby.

'My father talked to a couple of reporters—over there in some field or other, yesterday.'

'What did he say?' asked Michele.

'I don't really know. I only got there at the end.'

'But you were there, you were with him,' said Joan, in a transparent attempt at ingratiation. 'How nice! Because you've really had *very* little contact with your father in the past, haven't you? And now—practically his right-hand man!'

Raicho did not respond to this. He took a piece of toast and buttered it. The others looked at each other, forged into an *ad hoc* alliance by their common uncertainty.

'I don't see any harm in it,' said Chokey. 'Phil always was gabby.'

'I must say,' said Joan, 'that I don't think it was wise. After all, you know what reporters can *do* with what you say.'

'The *Grub* does it with what you don't say,' said Michele.

Suddenly Trevor pricked up his ears.

'That sounded like the phone.'

'Can't be,' said Chokey. 'They're all unplugged. I had to plug one in when I rang my bookmaker yesterday.'

'I think it was, though,' said Trevor. 'Perhaps someone forgot to pull it out.'

Mr Lillywaite had suggested — had almost, so dour was his manner, ordered — that the phone be disconnected. He had impressed on the family, and later on Phil during their walk together, the harm that could be done by one incautious word to the newspapers. When the police had begun to man the old, disused switchboard he had given them a brief statement to be read out to the press and to all other inquirers. But Mr Lillywaite's word, it seemed, was no longer law. When Phil had finished digesting the newspapers he had gone into the Great Hall and plugged in the phone.

'Switchboard? For the next few hours I'll take all calls that come in for the family. That's right: all calls.'

Then he had gone back into the Drawing-Room and waited. He had not had long to wait.

'Yes?' said Phil, when he picked up the phone. 'This *is* the Earl of Ellesmere . . . The *Clarion*? . . . No, I'm sorry I don't know of any new developments. I expect the rozzers will tell the papers quick enough if there are any . . No, I'm not giving any interviews until after this business is cleared up . . . After? Well, that's a different matter. It's quite possible I'll be willing to give interviews after that,

depending, of course, on the terms you're offering . . .
Well, you just run along to your Press lord and see what
he's willing to cough up, eh? And we'll talk about it later.'

The voice on the other end began jabbering further
questions, but Phil, with a pleased grin on his face, firmly
put down the phone. He turned round and saw gathered
at the end of the passage his brother, his sister, and most
of the other enforced residents at Chetton.

'That was the *Clarion*,' said Phil, and ambled back
towards the Drawing-Room. He had scarcely reached its
door when the telephone rang again.

'Chetton Hall . . . the Earl speaking . . . No, I've
nothing to add to what was in the *Grub* and *Telegram*
today . . . When things are sorted out we might have a
chat, if we can come to some arrangement—financial
arrangement, that is . . . I'm expecting the *Observer* to
send Kenneth Harris, so I'd want one of your top
men . . .'

And as Phil, exuding charm and intelligent concern,
strung the Press along, the assembled guests stood there,
gazing with wild surmise. Only Trevor chortled and
opined, as usual, that it was a right giggle.

By mid-morning Phil was getting exhausted. It wasn't
exactly that the charm was wearing thin, but it was
patently becoming more of an effort. Some little
cockneyism to each of the callers, some insubstantial
promise of jam tomorrow, some broad hint of the
necessity of paying for it—it all took mental effort. When
Mr Lillywaite rang to wring his hands, verbally, over the
material in that morning's papers, Phil cut him very short
indeed. He was quite pleased when he saw Raicho
returning from an interview with Superintendent
Hickory.

'How did it go?'

'Fine, Dad,' said Raicho laconically.

'What did you tell him?'

'The truth.'

'And nothing but the truth, I hope,' said Phil, un-accountably missing out 'the whole truth'. 'Look, I've got a little job for you. Oh good—here are the kids.'

Since the return of their father, and especially since the retreat into purdah of their mother, who had not been seen yet that day, the children had been running wild. Phil sent the younger two out to the grounds, to run a little wilder, and gathered Karen, Gareth and Raicho around the telephone.

'I'm pooped, so you lot are going to take over—right? The spiel is this: there won't be any statements or interview till after the police have finished their inquiries. After that I'll be considering all offers of interviews, if the terms are right. Anything else—opening bazaars, super-market, TV, radio, anything like that—tell them to put their offer in writing. I'll be dealing with all corres-pondence after the police—etcetera, etcetera, and so on. Anything unusual, you come to me and I'll deal with it. Got that?'

The phone rang as he spoke.

'Right. I'll take this last one, so listen carefully.'

He took up the receiver.

'Yes, this *is* Chetton Hall . . . Mr *Trevor* Spender? . . . Are you sure? . . . What was it you wanted to speak to him about? . . . Oh, I see . . . I dunno, but I'll see if he's available.'

He laid down the receiver, grimaced at the children, and shook his head. Then he went over to the Drawing-Room.

'Someone wants you on the buzzer, Trev. Some film company. And if it's an offer, try to keep your clothes on in this one, will you? For the honour of the family.'

'I never get offered roles like that,' said Trevor, getting up with alacrity.

'No, well, him at the other end didn't sound like Metro-Goldwyn-Mayer, I must admit. Make it brief, though, Trev. We don't want to hold up the flow.'

'Insist on something with a bit of *class*,' called Michele.

Phil was just about to slip into some unoccupied room and have a bit of rest and relaxation when he was arrested by a clumping sound on the stairs. Dixie was coming down. And since she had not been heard before she began descending, it was a fair bet that she'd been listening from the top. In her hand was a copy of the *Grub* which some kind person, perhaps knowing her likely reaction to the picture on the front page, had brought up to her bedroom. Ignoring Trevor's agitated signals to keep her voice down, she looked murderously at her husband, and said:

'What the hell do you think you're playing at, Phil?'

'Making us a bundle, I hope, Dixie. Any objections?'

'Why the blazes didn't you tell me about it?'

'But Dixie, you haven't been in talking mood since yesterday.'

'In the old days you wouldn't have dared . . .'

'Ah, the old days,' said Phil, and he walked into the Green Drawing-Room, rubbing his hands.

The family looked at him, with that expression of bemusement on their faces that Phil's activities had begun to arouse. They had sent into Chetton Lacey too, to get more papers, and the various accounts of the murder investigation were scattered around the tables and chairs. As Trevor's phone call ended, and he came in chortling with an almost innocent delight at his prospects in the dirty-raincoat cinema trade, the voice of Raicho could be heard from the Hall, answering the next call.

'No, my father won't be making any statement until . . .'

'Phil,' said Joan, 'we'd like to know—'

'Sorry, old girl, I'm up to my eyes,' said Phil.

'Sam—can you come and have a chat for a minute? I've got a job for you.'

And whether or not this was merely an excuse to avoid further questions, for half an hour after this Phil and Sam walked up and down the gravelly paths of the Dutch Garden, deep in conversation. Their every step was followed closely from the windows of the Green Drawing-Room.

Peter Medway had slept on the overnight ferry from Fishguard to Rosslare, and he felt sharp-minded and refreshed. It wasn't long before he felt he needed to be.

The two sergeants in the small town of Dungarvan who had arrested the wanted pair were a contrast of types: one was curly-headed, vocal, and could charm an ayatollah into a sex shop; the other was tall, raw-boned, and had one of those massive Irish chins that means that its possessor will be a great opera-singer or a great numskull. Or both.

'We really are enormously impressed,' said Medway. 'We didn't dare to hope for them to be taken anything like as quickly as this.'

'Surely it was nothin',' said Chucklehead airily. 'We do what we can to help the English *po*lice—if it's not political an' all.'

'It was on account of the swine fehver,' said Chin.

'I beg your pardon.'

'On account of the swine fehver. We was lookin' for pigs.'

'It's like this, y' see,' said Chucklehead. 'There's this bad attack of the fehver, up Limerick way, an' the eejuts up there will bring their little squealers out of the county to try an' save them—because the government's compensation's appallin'ly low. Thus spreadin' the sickness to the whole of the civilized globe, y' see. So we're mannin' this road block, see, an' we stop this ancient ve*hic*le—'

'Not seein' it was British, or we'd never have troubled—'

'No, not noticin' that, so that before you could say Cardinal MacFeogh we've opened up the back, put their luggage on the road, and pulled up the back seat—'

'Because that's where the little darlin's often hide themselves.'

'An' what do we find but this handsome bit of oil paintin', and a clock the like of which the Taoiseach himself hasn't got on his mantelpiece. All under the seat. So we think it's a bit suspicious, like, an' as how it might not be all above board. An' so we have this pair out of the car, and we tump them about a bit—'

'Tump?'

'That's right, we tump them about a bit, but all they say is they've no idea them things was there, an' they must have been planted, if y'd believe it. So we bring them back here, and we wonders if there's anythin' come from England about an old cream Escort.'

' 'Twas your idea entirely,' said Chin admiringly.

'You'd have thought of it yourself eventually, Eamon. So when we find as how there was, we get on the line to Waterford, and there y' are.'

'Well, we're very grateful to you,' said Peter Medway, feeling less strong than when he had arrived. 'I think it might be a good idea if I saw them now.'

'Sure you can, an' with pleasure. They're a snooty pair, an' no great fun to have around, so if you *can* arrange a spot of extradition, we wouldn't be cryin' any bitther tears.'

And when Peter Medway got to talk to Parsloe and Nazeby, he sensed they wouldn't be grieved to be out of there either. Parsloe, in fact, seemed to breathe a sigh of relief at the sight of a British uniform. He was a fleshy man of middle height, with dark, slicked-back hair. In normal circumstances his impressive manner would stop you noticing the weak mouth, the slight air of going to seed. Nazeby was good-looking, thirtyish, with hard lines about the mouth and clear hazel eyes. Normally she would probably have a competent, slightly bossy air, and of the two she certainly seemed the more dangerous. Now both of them looked driven, off-centre; both were grubby, and Parsloe was bruised.

'Look,' said the butler, looking straight at Peter Medway as if sizing him up, 'I know what you've come for, and we'd better tell you what we told that precious pair out there. We recognize those things they found in the car—of course we do. They come from Chetton. But we had no idea they were there, not a notion in the world. Having blotted our copy-book with staying on there, we'd naturally be doubly careful. They must have been planted.'

'Well, that's as maybe. You'd better tell me how you left Chetton.'

'It was about half past six on the Sunday morning. We didn't want any unpleasantness. We don't make any bones about it: we shouldn't have been there. But when the Earl said we had to go, we went at once.'

'When you think,' said Nazeby, who did seem inclined to make bones, 'of what these hippie squatters get away with.'

'And we did no harm at all to the house. We cleaned up so well you wouldn't know we'd been there. But it was wrong, we admit it. Still, the idea of stealing anything from the house: we simply wouldn't have contemplated it.'

'Hmmm,' said Peter Medway. 'The fact remains that you left Chetton shortly after the murder of the Earl, in possession of items of his property—wittingly or not. That puts you in a pretty serious position.'

'We realize that,' said Nazeby, in her hard, managerial voice. 'But we've talked it over, and we've decided to go back of our own accord.'

'Ah!' said Medway, brightening. He hadn't fancied facing all the rigmaroles of extradition procedures, particularly in the company of the pair of comedians in the outer office. 'That certainly will make matters simpler.'

'We'll just have to hope,' said Parsloe, 'that the British police are as fair and thorough as they're supposed to be.'

He didn't sound at all convinced they were.

'Quite apart from anything else,' said Nazeby, whose decision this obviously was, 'we'd never get another job, not with this hanging over us.'

'I think you're very wise,' said Medway.

'God only knows what might happen to us if we stayed here,' muttered Parsloe.

'Quite,' agreed Sergeant Medway. 'My guess is you'd be put down — on account of the swine fehver.'

At the end of the afternoon Phil was jubilant.

'Well,' he said to the trio who had manned the phone, 'that was a day and a half! You've done a job to be proud of. You two can go out now and play — and I'll slip you something when I have a spot of the ready. I'll unplug the phone soon, so we can get a bit of peace and quiet this evening.' He poked his head into the Drawing-Room. 'Hey, Trevor, what do you think of this: five supermarket openings, one prize-giving at a Comprehensive, seven bazaars and a feeler whether I'd like to be on *Any Questions?* You're not the only one in the public eye any longer. By tomorrow they'll be asking me to turn on the Christmas lights in Regent Street.'

Dixie, a mountainous load of flesh and discontent in her usual chair over by the windows, stared at her husband with an expression hardly less lethal than it had been that morning.

'*What* the hell are you playing at, Phil?' she asked again.

'I'm becoming a personality, Dixie. You know, the sort of bloke everybody recognizes, even though he doesn't do anything in particular. Don't you think I have the makings of a personality, Dixie?'

Dixie considered, glowering. When she spoke it was on another subject entirely.

'I told you to keep that bastard of yours out of my sight.'

'Raicho? Can't do that. Raicho's my right-hand man.'

Dixie cast at Raicho a look that comprised a whole armoury of daggers, then she muttered, 'If you don't get rid of him, watch out I don't,' and stomped out of the room and up the stairs, arrested only by Phil's parting shot:

'Oh, Dixie: be careful how you use that word "bastard". He's not, you know. And it's a word you ought to be sensitive about.'

Dixie's choke of outrage was interrupted by the telephone, and Phil, with an amused shrug of the shoulders at his burgeoning popularity, went out to the Hall to take it.

'Chetton Hall . . . Yes, this is the Earl . . . Who? . . . Oh, Sir Gerald Dowley. Would that be of Brycenorton Towers? Yes, I've heard of the place . . . No, we haven't so far had the pleasure.' At the other end Sir Gerald launched into an elaborate apology for their previous ignorance of each other's existence, as if it was surprising they hadn't met up in some dinky little pub near the Billingsgate Fish Market. Phil listened with a tolerant expression, and when the fluent conventionalities showed signs of slowing down, cut in with an 'Equally so. I'll hope to make your acquaintance before too long, Sir Gerald. Is there anything I can do for you now? . . . Well, that's very nice of you . . . Neighbourly. I appreciate it very much . . . Matter of fact, there are a couple of things I'd like to chew over with you . . . Now? I don't know what the cops would say to that. Perhaps if they could spare a man to drive me. You wouldn't object to that? . . . No, what I say is, cops are almost as human as the rest of us . . . Well, if you'll just hang on a minute I'll see what they say.'

Phil put down the phone, grinned at Raicho, and muttered, 'Starting to get in with the local nobs.' Then he ambled over to the nearest policeman and sent him off to get permission from Hickory. Soon he came back to the phone.

'Sir Gerald? Yes, I've okayed it with the law. They want to talk to me later, so I guess something's turned up, but it's in order for an hour or two. The police driver will know the way, I suppose. Be with you in as long as it takes.'

He put down the phone.

'That's what I like about the aristocracy in this country. No side. As long as you've got the dibs they welcome you with open arms. Watch out for yourself while I'm gone, Raicho. What I'd suggest is a long walk in a nice open field, with a cop nearby.'

Phil hugely enjoyed his visit to Brycenorton Towers. After the police driver had been dispatched to the kitchen quarters, watched sardonically by Phil, Sir Gerald and Lady Dowley sat the new Earl down in a comfortable old armchair, offered him a drink ('Anything that's going,' said Phil) and made him very welcome, rather as they might the postman at Christmas time. When they had gone through the condolences, and made the ritual noises of welcome to a new member of the landed classes, Sir Gerald asked Phil what it was he wanted to talk over with him.

'Well, it's this matter of house security,' said Phil. 'O'

course, I know a bit about it, but that's from the other side of the fence, as it were.'

Sir Gerald laughed a fruity, landowner's laugh, and Lady Dowley leaned forward.

'You're thinking of opening to the public, then?'

'Well, it's going through my mind, yes.'

'Good. The old Earl kept the place *much* too closed, for one of our great houses.'

'That's what I thought. No disrespect, but from what I can gather even them eighteenth-century blokes were more willing to let people in for a dekko.'

'You'll find plenty of problems on your plate, though,' said Sir Gerald with relish, and he launched into an exposition of those problems. It was a subject that was very close to his heart. He explained that thieves had broken into Brycenorton earlier in the year, aiming at its superb china collection, and since then he prided himself that the house had been made burglar-proof, or as nearly so as any old place could be. He went into detail on the circumstances of the robbery (which Phil seemed to enjoy) and on all the measures taken, the devices fitted, the redeployment of the attendants. Phil took it all in, and even made the odd note.

'It's like this,' said Phil at the end; 'it seems to me that, with the old bloke keeping the place so closed, there must be thousands of connoisseurs just itching to have a peep at it. Not to mention the ghouls—after all this. And what I thought was: Lillywaite says there's no way I can keep the house. OK, he should know. But it's going to be years before the dear old Chancellor puts in his bill. Just think of making an up-to-date inventory of all the stuff in there—and that's before they start putting a price on everything, and before I start quibbling and quarrelling and entering into negotiations. Get the idea? It could take five years, easy. Meanwhile, anything I make out of the place is mine, by my reckoning. And my guess is, I'd make a bomb.'

'You could be right,' said Sir Gerald. 'It's a thought.'

'And then there was this joker in the House, yesterday, with his obliging suggestion, which tickled me pink. So, all in all, there seem to be various possibilities opening up.'

So they chewed over these and other matters, and had a couple more drinks, and when Phil had collected his driver from the kitchens he invited his hosts over to Chetton 'when all this bovver's cleared up', and he said he'd welcome Sir Gerald's opinion as to which rooms at Chetton could most easily be opened to the public 'without them getting their thieving hands on anything of value'. He left in an aura of goodwill ('Quite a card,' said Sir Gerald to his lady, 'but somehow basically sound, didn't you feel?'), and he sat out the drive back to Chetton in deep thought. The journalists at the gate were much augmented in numbers since the success of the *Grub* and *Telegram* men the day before, but Phil ignored them. He jumped out of the car in the courtyard, and went straight along to have his talk with Hickory.

'Tatty old room you picked here,' he said, looking around the Pink Damask Room. 'Looks like a high-class knocking shop — and, my ancestresses being what they were, that's probably what it was.'

'Wouldn't have been my choice,' said Hickory apologetically, gazing round with his glum, farmer's expression of never expecting anything but the worst. 'I just sort of landed up here. Well, I thought I'd better tell you the news: there's two people arrested in Ireland, and my man has just confirmed that they are Parsloe and Nazeby, and that in their car were several items from this house.'

Phil looked at him, frowning.

'Really? What were they doing in Ireland? You don't hook it to Ireland. Once you're there there's nowhere else

to go. Quite apart from all the security checks against the
IRA and that mob.'

'They were on their way to a new job there, in County
Cork. They were arrested at a place called Dungarvan.'

Phil looked at him acutely.

'That doesn't figure, and you know it doesn't. Not with
the murder. They might have thought they could get
away with filching a few odds and sods from the house,
but if they'd done the murder they'd never have gone
calmly off to a new job without ditching the stuff.'

'The thought had occurred to me,' said Hickory.
'We're not entirely ignorant of the criminal mind, in the
Force. At the moment I'm regarding this pair as a piece in
the jigsaw—nothing more. But I thought you'd like to
know.'

'Thanks a million,' said Phil. 'You got any ideas when
this mob can get away from here? They're my family, and
I love them very much, mostly, but there's an atmosphere
out there like Hitler's bunker in April 'forty-five.'

'I rather gathered that from my sergeant. You seem to
have kept up your spirits, though.'

'Oh, me—I'm the original cockney sparrow.'

Hickory sighed. He was finding Phil more than ever an
enigma.

'Well, obviously I can't keep them indefinitely. You'd
better tell them that once I've talked to Parsloe and
Nazeby I'll go over their stories with them once more, and
then they'll be free to go. Say Friday. Provided, of course,
we can be quite sure of getting hold of them again,
whenever we want to.'

'Right!' said Phil. 'That should mean a let-up in the
Cold War. And Mum will be pleased.'

'And you too, I suppose?'

'Well, natch. Family's all very well, but taken in a
lump, and jumpy as they are, they're a right bind.'

'What I really meant was that you couldn't feel entirely

safe, with them all around you.'

Phil grinned.

' "The curse of the Spenders strikes again," ' he said. 'Oh, I can look after myself. Besides, you might say that Raicho is my defence policy.' He went on, unconsciously echoing Charles II: 'Nobody around here's going to kill me to make Raicho Earl.'

'That's a dangerous game, Lord Ellesmere,' said Hickory, in his gravelly voice. 'What about the boy himself?'

'Oh, I'm keeping an eye on Raicho. No harm's going to come to him.'

'That wasn't what I meant.'

'If you mean that Raicho may have done it, you're barking up the wrong Canadian pine, mate,' said Phil with spirit.

'Meaning you know which tree I should be barking up?'

'No, no. I wouldn't say that.' Phil had got up, and had strolled to the door. 'Mind you, what you say is right in a way. I shouldn't feel too safe. When you think of it, there have been an awful lot of Earls of Ellesmere dying in the last few months, haven't there? Ever thought of getting a statistician on to the chances against? Ever thought it might be worth looking into some of the other deaths?'

CHAPTER 14

THE DUTCH GARDEN

'Phil,' said Elsie, Dowager Countess of Ellesmere, 'I want to go home.'

It was the Thursday morning, and the sun, though shining, appeared through a thin haze that made things altogether cooler and pleasanter outside. Breakfast had

been the usual uneasy affair, the more so as Dixie had put
in an appearance. Raicho also came down, looking very
scrubbed and fresh, and smelling of after-shave. When he
saw Dixie he blenched somewhat, but he was with Phil
and he kept close to him, and in the course of the meal he
seemed to gain confidence, addressing several remarks to
his father, whom he always called Dad—perhaps because
children brought up by their mothers do feel the need to
emphasize their relationship with their father, perhaps as
a sort of declaration for Dixie's benefit. Dixie responded
no further than to make a demonstrative show of
affection for her own children, but even this she gave up
when Cliff said: 'What are you doing *that* for?' from the
depths of one of her mountainous embraces.

Afterwards they all drifted out into the Dutch Garden
and fetched chairs of one sort or another, perhaps to
make it clear to Phil that they had no stomach for another
day of strenuous physical activity. Joan sat decorously in a
deckchair while Digby leaned over the back, talking
quietly and seriously. Trevor sprawled on his chair, while
Michele wafted herself down to the fountain, removed
her dress while those on the terrace ostentatiously bated
their breaths, and then sunbathed, topless and
bottomless, on the chill flagstones. 'Christ, Trev, you do
pick 'em,' said Phil, but he sat on the balustrade and
surveyed her appreciatively. Dixie prowled, Sam sat
astride the balustrade, writing assiduously, and Chokey
kept coming up to Phil with little reminiscences of the old
days—perhaps to reassure himself of their intimacy,
perhaps for the view afforded of Michele beneath them,
wriggling luxuriously at the sensual contrast of warm sun
and cold stone.

It was while they were whiling away the morning thus
that the Countess came out to them, her bulk covered by
the grubby blue dressing-gown she always wore at this
time of day, the hair around each ear caught up in the

two obligatory curlers.

'Phil,' she said, 'I want to go home. I don't like this place. I never have, and Perce dying here—*look* at that hussey! The nerve!—Perce dying here makes me hate the very feel of it. Horrible, shivery old dump! I don't think them coppers would object, do you?'

'I don't think so, Ma. I talked to them yesterday.'

'I don't like leaving Perce down here, but he'd have understood. He knew how I felt—I made sure of that! We'll have him back home when the police say we can.'

'You'd like him buried in Clapham, would you?'

The Countess stared at him, outraged.

'Are you out of your mind, Phil? O' course I'm going to have him buried in Clapham. You wouldn't want me to leave him down here in some old family vault, would you? Shoved on a bleeding shelf, next to that old buzzard who never once acknowledged his existence in all the sixty years he was alive. Not on your life. Perce didn't owe nothing to his family, and he wouldn't want to lie with them. I'm going to see about a nice little plot by the Duffield Street Methodist Chapel.'

'Dad was a Methodist, was he?'

' 'Course he was, when he thought about it.'

'Well, that's OK by me, Ma. I thought that'd be what you'd prefer.'

'And what he'd prefer too. Will you speak to the policeman, Phil?'

'I spoke to him yesterday. I'm pretty sure it will be all right. Digby could drive you up, if you went tomorrow, or Trevor could hire a car. I think the Super will agree to everyone going.'

There were stirrings from deckchairs and pathways. Digby, who had moved over to talk to Sam and was trying to get a look at what he was writing, straightened and walked over. Joan and Trevor turned in their deckchairs to look in Phil's direction, and Dixie stopped in her tracks

and stared at him. Raicho, perched on the balustrade
with his chin in his knees, watched Phil intently with his
veiled eyes.

'Yes,' said Phil, 'I think he'll be agreeable to you all
pushing off.'

They all seemed to be torn both ways. To be gone
would be a relief in one way, but to go while still unsure of
Phil's intentions would be deeply unsatisfactory.

'Does that mean he realizes it was none of us?' asked
Joan.

'Couldn't say, love.'

'I'd give him what-for if he suspected *me*,' said the
Countess.

'Nobody's ever suspected you, Ma,' said Phil, putting
his arm around her. 'All I know is, they've got hold of this
butler and cook, and they're turning off the heat.'

That news, at least, went down well.

'I always said it was funny about them,' said Chokey.

'Stands to reason they're the most likely,' said Joan.

'And will you be staying down here, Phil?' asked
Trevor.

'Natch. There's all these newspaper interviews and
television spots I'm lining up for myself. Got a whole wad
of offers in the post today. There wouldn't be much point
if they weren't done at Chetton.'

'Michele and me could use a bit of publicity. You could
cut us in on the action.'

'If I know you two, Trevor, you'll cut yourselves in on
the action, one way or another.'

'Before he cuts you in,' came Dixie's aggressive voice, 'it
might be nice if he cut his wife in. Apparently he goes
visiting among classy neighbours and I don't get to go
along.'

'They didn't invite you, Dixie, so I suppose they never
heard of you. Your fame hasn't penetrated to this neck of
the woods.'

'It'd be nice to know whether I figure in any of the future action. Seems to me I'm to be kept under wraps.'

'Dixie, he'd be a brave man who tried to keep you under wraps. Look, we'll make a bargain: if I get any requests to compère fashion shows, I'll hand them straight over to you.' He paused. From the distance there came the wheeze and phut of an elderly vehicle. 'Listen. Some old banger's driving into the courtyard. What's the betting it's Jeeves and his floozie? Who knows—they may have the key to the whole business.'

Superintendent Hickory, massively settled into his spindly desk chair, surveyed the newly-arrived suspects at unnerving and silent length. They shifted uneasily in the Sheraton chairs of the Pink Damask Room. Both of them had spruced themselves up, Nazeby decidedly so, but they still gave off an aura of acute unease, like two dogs sitting beside a chewed rug.

'Well, now,' said Hickory at length, 'perhaps we can take as read all the stuff about how you regret staying on, how you're thoroughly ashamed of what you did—or, in your case, Miss Nazeby, not particularly ashamed. You've been over this with Sergeant Medway, and it's not what I'm interested in. Now, before we get down to the serious bit, let's try and fill in the background a little. How did you live in the weeks you camped here?'

'How did we live?' said Parsloe, his voice unnaturally high. 'Well, we'd got in a stock of food, and what else we needed we bought in the evenings from the shop in Chetton. It's open all hours.'

'I see. You went out at nights.'

'That's right. Nipped out from one of the doors in the wing, took the car—it's mine—and then went into Chetton Lacey or further afield. Had a drink somewhere or other, and bought what we needed. We had a Post Office box number, and Jack at the Chetton Arms

ollected our mail. So we got in job particulars, sent in
ur applications, and waited till we got one we felt like
ccepting. We weren't going to jump at the first one, just
ecause we happened to be out of work.'

'The locals kept mum about you?'

'Of course they did,' said Parsloe, relaxing a little.
I've been here five years, Betty three. We're almost locals
urselves. They looked on the Earl as a sort of day
ripper.'

'Mind you,' said Betty Nazeby, who got restive when
'arsloe did most of the talking, 'he nearly caught us once.
Came in when Bill was drinking in the Chetton Arms.
The locals had a good laugh about that, next evening.
The Earl kept going on about how he wasn't used to
ervants in the house, and they kept mum and had a good
iggle when he and the Countess were gone.'

'I begin to get the picture,' said Hickory heavily. 'What
id you do otherwise?'

'What was there to do? We had the telly up there, but
n the daytime there's nothing but bloody nature pro-
rammes and keep fit classes. We became night birds—
ead and slept a lot during the day, perked up at night.'

'Where did you get the books from?'

'From here, mostly. We had the run of the house at
ight. The books in the library are mostly musty old
arbage, but there's a lot of reasonable stuff in the old
Earl's study. He didn't belong to a library, naturally, but
e ordered anything that took his fancy from Hatchard's.
Travel, biography, thrillers—we must have read the
omplete Desmond Bagley.'

'You say you fetched the books at night?'

'That's it. Once the Earl and Countess—Perce and
Elsie we called them to ourselves—had gone to bed, we
ad the freedom of the whole house, just as we'd always
ad in the past. We had to remember to be very quiet
vhen we went past the State Bedroom, because Perce was

a light sleeper. Came out once and switched on lights when he heard the stairs creak. Luckily we know the house like the backs of our hands, so we could always find somewhere to hide.'

'Mind you,' said Nazeby, who was also thawing and relaxing visibly, 'there was once we got a nasty shock. It was just before we got found out. We knew Perce and Elsie had visitors, because we'd seen the cars—'

'One of them down by the fountain,' said Parsloe sententiously. 'Can you imagine?'

'—but we didn't realize how *many* people there were around. We were just making our way through the wing when we heard a door·open. We slipped into the clock room, and waited till whoever it was went past.'

'The clock room?'

'But we *didn't*—' began Parsloe.

'No, no. Well, let's come to the business of your leaving. You were caught—when?—Saturday night.'

'I wouldn't say we were *caught*,' said Nazeby. 'By then we just didn't care. We had a job to go to anyway. When we heard this frightful din, with them dancing all round the place and singing some incredible song . . . one doesn't want to be snobbish, but *really* . . . Bill wanted to turn off the lights, but I said,"No, what the hell?" because it would have been worse if we'd been caught crouching in the dark.'

'I think I'd have chanced the crouching,' said Hickory. 'What did you do on the Saturday night, after you'd been caught?'

'Well,' said Nazeby, swallowing, 'after the Earl ordered us out—Christ, he was in a bate! The old Earl would never have dared to speak to us like that—after that, we had a drink, a stiff one, and had a bit of a laugh about it all. Bill's way of dealing with them had been a treat!'

'It was a trifle ludicrous,' said Parsloe, with a touch of

his butlerian manner, 'being discovered by a hokey-kokey party.'

'And then?'

'Well, over the drink we decided to go to Ireland earlier than we'd planned. Bill thought it would be cheap there, and I didn't know any better. Have we found out since! Anyway, we'd have liked to ring to see if the ferry from Fishguard was full, but we thought there wouldn't be any booking-place open at that time, and anyway the nearest telephone extension was in the library, and we knew by then that there were people sleeping in the Blenheim Wing. So we just packed up, cleaned up the room, and then we thought we'd make sure of our route. But our map of Wales and the West was in the car.'

'Ah! You went out!'

'Yes. Nobody could object to that, that we could see.' Nazeby's chin went up, as if she were permanently on the scent for opposition. 'There's a door out at the end of the Wing. We were very quiet and went out that way.'

'Was it locked?'

'Yes, of course. We had keys.'

'Did you lock it while you were gone?'

'Well—no, we didn't actually,' said Parsloe, whose job the locking up had always been. 'I mean, it's only three or four minutes to the stables.'

'In the dark?' queried Hickory. 'Quite a bit more, I'd have thought.'

'There was a moon. We knew the grounds as well as we knew the house. We'd often come back that way on our nights out.'

'It was creepy, though,' admitted Betty Nazeby. 'Shadows. I thought I saw someone.'

'Oh, did you? And was it anyone?'

Nazeby creased her forehead.

'I just don't know. I've thought about it, but I can't decide. With all those long shadows . . . At the time I thought it might be one of the guests, but Bill said I was drunk.'

'Where was this shadow?'

'Not far from the stables. I felt it went in the direction of the big oak—Dick Mont's oak, they call it—which is about ten yards away. But it could have been a squirrel or something, I must admit.'

'You didn't see anything else, or hear anything?'

'No, there wasn't anything else. Oh, except—'

'Yes?'

'When we opened the car, Bill thought . . . he said he smelt perfume. Quite strongly. But it could have been me.'

'All you were smelling of was whisky,' said Parsloe. 'No, I did think I smelt it. But it might have been something Betty left in the car. We'd been out in it the night before. Powder compact. Scent, perhaps.'

'I don't think I left anything there. I'm pretty careful like that.'

Hickory surveyed them thoughtfully. Was this a tale they'd dreamed up together in Dungarvan, to give substance to their story that the loot had been planted on them? Or was it truth? If it was a piece of collusion, surely they'd have made it a bit more substantial? If it was truth, it was very interesting indeed. Because, surely, if the stuff *was* planted on them, it would have to have been planted between the discovery of them during the party and their departure in the early morning.

'Anything else you remember from that night?' he asked.

'No, I don't think so,' said Parsloe. 'We locked the car, went back in, got back to our room without being seen, and went over our route over another glass of whisky. Then we turned in for a few hours' sleep. Got up about six or so, had a snack, then I drove the car round to the door at the rear end of the Wing, we piled the luggage in, and I drove off.'

'And the first you knew of the loot was when the Irish police discovered it under the seat?'

'Of course it was. Why would we take up the back seat?'

'Why, indeed? Why would anyone—unless they were looking for IRA arms, or pigs with the swine fever. I must say I think you're an unappetizing pair, but your story has this to commend it: if I was making off with stolen property, the last route on earth I'd take would be the sea route to Ireland.'

Hickory sent them back in custody to Meresham, and then sat in his unsuitable little chair, sunk in agricultural meditation.

Mr Lillywaite made his reappearance in the afternoon. He had not been idle. He had been consulting here, dropping a word there, sounding out the lie of the land elsewhere. Burrowing, constructing unobtrusive earth-works—these were activities that came naturally to Mr Lillywaite. All, it goes without saying, in the interests of his clients. Now he talked to Phil in the late afternoon sun of the Dutch Garden. Some of the party were now inside, packing or prospecting around for the last time. Trevor, though, had taken his deckchair down to the fountain, and Michele lay more spectacularly beside him, as if auditioning for the part of the corpse. Mr. Lillywaite took off his spectacles, cast a glance of Presbyterian outrage at her, said 'Tchah', and then looked determinedly the other way.

'Lord Ellesmere,' he said, keeping his voice low, 'I've been talking to your neighbours, the Dowleys.'

'I thought you might,' said Phil.

'And I've been reading the papers. As I said to you on the telephone yesterday, I think you have been wise. However, I begin to perceive some plan, some method . . . Am I right?'

'Could be,' said Phil.

'I wish you had consulted me first.'

'I've been developing the plan as I go. Anyway, it was a fair bet you wouldn't approve.'

'I can't pretend that I do. Nevertheless, it has certain points in its favour. I cannot imagine, though, that the financial dividends you might reap would be such that you could hold on to the house.'

'For the moment, all I'm aiming at is staving off the evil hour. The possibilities are endless: me and the kids can do cocoa ads if the money's right. Then the next line of retreat might involve following up that obliging suggestion from the MP the other day.'

'Yes,' said Mr Lillywaite, drawing in breath. 'I read about that.'

'Isn't it marvellous? Makes me glad I've always voted Labour—when I've been at liberty to. You and me'd better talk this over when the family's gone. I may as well tell you now that I'm going to open this house to the public.'

'Yes. I gathered that from Sir Gerald. I see nothing wrong with the plan. It is what I would have advised myself.'

'I'm going to open it the moment the police get their big boots out of the door, and I'm going to keep it open all summer at ten quid a head.'

'*What?*'

'Ten quid. I'll drop it when we open properly next spring. What we're going to get now will be the ghoul trade: they'll want to gape at the scene of the crime, catch a glimpse of the gaolbird Earl all the papers have been going on about. OK—then they'll have to pay for it. Through the nose. I'm getting a series of interviews lined up to fan the interest, and as many personal appearances as I can cram in. There'll be queues from the Great Entrance to the Main Gate.'

'But, Lord Ellesmere,' said Mr Lillywaite, with an expression of acute disgust on his cavernous face, 'surely it would be distasteful to you to *capitalize* on a family tragedy in that way?'

'Stick me to the heart. Still, Dad wasn't squeamish. I'll beg his pardon when we're both on the same side of the pearly gates. He'll understand when I tell him what the takings were.'

'Oh dear, oh dear,' murmured Mr Lillywaite. 'I see, I begin to see, what you have in mind. But I don't like it. I don't like it at all.'

'In that case, you'll just have to lump it, old cock,' said Phil.

'It was a perfectly good story, so far as it went,' said Hickory to Peter Medway when, in the evening, they found themselves together in the Pink Damask Room. They stood looking at the attractive Cotman that had been found in the car, at the rather florid clock, and at the collection of toilet jars and jewellery, some of it superb, some very ordinary.

'It's a very random collection of stuff,' said Hickory. 'But then it would be if they just grabbed what was conveniently to hand on their last night here.'

'But on the whole you believe their story, don't you, sir?'

'Yes. Because though I can see them as capable of robbing the house—Nazeby especially, out of spite—I just can't see them trolling off to Ireland afterwards. If she'd decided to rob the place, Nazeby would have got a much bigger haul, and she'd have been off to the Continent. The difficulties in the way of a murder charge are even greater: no jury is going to believe that after robbing the house and murdering the Earl this pair would calmly proceed to their next job, with the loot very superficially concealed, still in the car. They wouldn't believe it, and I don't.'

'No. It seems incredibly stupid, and I don't get the impression that Nazeby is stupid in the least. Anything come up while I was in Ireland?'

'We've got a fair bit on this Raicho character. Tallies with what he told us. He had spent the last few months in Europe, then he had ten days in Canada before flying to England. He said he returned to Canada because he was on a special cheap ticket that included the fare back, and that's true. What he didn't tell us was that he only booked for his Monday flight to England on Sunday night. Make what you like of that. He went straight from Heathrow to Phil's home in Stepney. Talked to the neighbours, was shown Monday's evening papers with the picture of you and Phil leaving gaol, expressed great surprise and interest. Came down here on Tuesday—rail to Meresham, bus to the gates of Chetton, the rest we know.'

'It is odd that he should go back to Canada, then hot-foot it back to Europe. No point in taking up your cheap seat if you then have to fork out for a seat back.'

'Unless . . . oh well, just a thought. Gleaned anything from the constables about what the family's been up to while you've been in Ireland?'

'Trying to pin Phil down on what he's going to do for them. Want to get something definite before they push off.'

'You know, I do sometimes wonder about the Spenders.'

'Wonder, sir?'

'Wonder whether *all* the Spenders, and *all* their friends, and *all* their connections could have been quite so stupendously ignorant as they pretend of their position next in line to a whacking great fortune like this . . . And there's another thing.'

'What's that, sir?'

'There's one member of this cast list who doesn't add up.'

At that moment there was a knock on the door, and the burly head and shoulders of Phil poked themselves round.

'Him!' said Hickory. 'Come in, Lord Ellesmere, I was just talking about you. You're on my mind. I was just wondering whether crooks' ethics prevented your working with the police, and if that's why you've been playing the cat that walked on his own.'

'Watch your language, matey. Now I've served my time I'm pure as the driven snow. It's like going to confession. And I've been walking on my own because I've been out of things for three years, and I wanted to make sure my guesses were right.'

'Well, you've had four days to play your little games. Isn't it time now that we sat down and went at things together? Isn't it time you came completely clean?'

'Just what I'd decided myself,' said Phil.

CHAPTER 15

THE DINING-ROOM

On the day of her departure, the Countess found that her eager anticipation of going home was slightly dampened by her fear of ridicule, or worse.

'There's some as'll take the mickey,' she announced, in her doomsday-tomorrow voice, 'and more as would like to if they dared. My not using the title won't stop 'em. Mrs Parsons three doors down will be thinking up sarky remarks already, but I'll soon put *her* down. There'll be some as want to make Remarks, too. About Perce's death. Mrs Carter would be common enough, for one. I shall just say nothing. Maintain a dignified silence. Freeze her. All the same, I do wish it was all cleared up.'

The Countess, unusually for her so early in the day, was dressed. Indeed, she probably would have put on her coat and hat and sat with her case in the Hall if Phil had not dissuaded her. Phil had been in consultation again with the Superintendent during the morning, and had gathered that the final interviews would be finished by lunch-time. He had decided, with the Superintendent's approval, to give them all a slap-up meal before they departed. The Countess had declined the offer of a lift from Joan and Digby, and Trevor had gone off to Meresham to fetch a hire car in which to drive her home. Trevor was financially buoyed up by yesterday's offer of a film part in a homosexual skin-flick with a Japanese slant, to be called *Sayonara, Cheeky*.

'No offence, Joanie, but I'll let Trevor drive me, even if the trollop does come along,' the Countess explained to her daughter. 'After all, he does live at home, when he *is* at home.'

Phil asked for volunteers to help with the lunch. Dixie stared stonily ahead of her. Joan said she'd come down later, but she had an *awful* lot of packing to do first. Michele just said 'Are you out of your mind? I can't boil a bleeding egg.' In the end it was Raicho, coming from his second interview with the Superintendent, who found himself commandeered.

Once the two of them had settled down in the kitchen, they found they had plenty to talk about. While they chatted Phil put on the two large pork roasts he had got from the butcher in Chetton. Phil had driven in himself (such was now his standing with the investigating policemen that they had made no objections), pursued by yelping newsmen who photographed through the plate glass the homely spectacle of the new Earl being handed two substantial roasts over the counter, and of his not paying for them. Word had got around that the Earl, barring accidents such as his arrest for murder, was probably going to be around at Chetton for some time, and this had done wonders for the service. The butcher was positively oleaginous, and almost over-ready to put everything on account.

When the roast was sizzling Phil and Raicho set to on a positive mountain of potatoes. Raicho proved inexpert but willing. When Sergeant Medway poked his nose around the door he was conscripted to help. And when a thought occurred to Phil that he wanted to chew over with the Superintendent, he gave Medway strict instructions not to leave Raicho. 'Just to be on the safe side,' he said. When he returned he was thoughtful, and remained so during the rest of the preparations.

At one o'clock the interviews had all been completed. The luggage was standing in little piles near the Great Entrance, containing all the personal things the guests had brought to Chetton, and the little souvenirs they had decided to take away from it. Phil despatched Peter Medway with an armful of knives and forks to the Dining-Room, where the cloth was still on from the evening of the guests' arrival, together with much of the magnificent silver impedimenta of that meal. For this final lunch, though, Phil had resolved to make one change: the children could have a table to themselves down in the kitchen, so he told Medway to set places only for the adult members of the family, and for himself.

'The family won't want me eating with them,' said Peter Medway. 'Blight on the occasion. I'll stand near the door.'

'Not a bit of it,' said Phil. 'You're practically one of us by now. Just take your tie off, open the top button of your shirt, and nobody will notice you're not a slob like the rest of us.'

It was when they were about to serve out that Mr Lillywaite arrived. He had come in high expectation, having been summoned by Phil for the business discussion he had been waiting for. But in the event he found himself sat down at table between Lady Joan and the Countess, protesting bleakly that he had already eaten. When the family had all gathered in the Dining-Room, Phil and Raicho did a high-speed serving job in the kitchen, with Raicho serving the vegetables while Phil (who had often helped Mario, the Italian chef at Daintree) whipped through the carving with an almost professional air. Gravy came from a packet, but as Phil said: if no one was willing to chip in and help, they couldn't bleeding well complain. Finally Peter Medway did an expert waiting job with the plates, and the children were left tucking in in the kitchen, while upstairs everyone was wielding a moderately enthusiastic knife and fork. There was Lady Joan, making genteel conversation with the family man of law; there was Dixie heaving food muscularly into her substantial frame; there was Michele, toying wispily with her food, and there was Sam going at it with infectious enjoyment. There were, in fact, all the Spenders and their guests, with Phil bonhomous and hostly at the head of the table.

'Well,' he said, echoing his father six days before, 'this is nice.'

'Brings things back,' said the Countess, sniffing.

'Now then, Ma, have a bit of crackling and forget your troubles. You're going home now, aren't you? Just what you wanted, no place like it, and all that.'

'I wish I wasn't leaving you here. You won't like it, Phil whatever you may think now.'

'Don't you worry, Ma. I'm used to big places with hundreds of room. We're going to have a whale of a time here, I can tell you: a monster-sized giggle, as Trev would say.'

'*If* this 'ere business is ever seen the end of,' said the Countess gloomily.

'Oh, it will be, don't you worry, Ma. The Super has it well in hand, hasn't he, Peter?' Phil looked at Sergeant Medway. 'The Sergeant says that things are beginning to sort themselves out. And, anyway, we've done our bit. Everyone's been along to see the Super for the second time, haven't they? Mr Lillywaite excepted, naturally.'

'I thought it a waste of time,' said Joan, looking around the table from over her pretty apple-green blouse. 'And so did Digby. We could only tell him what we told him before. It doesn't seem to us as if he's getting *anywhere*.'

'It's like doing the same scene over and over again,' agreed Trevor, who was fitting in with the decor in a frilly white silken shirt and dark trousers. ' "Where were you on the night of Saturday the twenty-first?" "I was in bed, mostly asleep." Do it twenty times and get it perfect. I suppose you could say the old haystack was thorough, but he wasn't asking anything he hadn't asked before, so I don't suppose he's got any new information. I agree with Joan: unless he's just marking time till he claps the handcuffs on that butler and his girl, it seems as if he's getting nowhere fast.'

'Oh, you don't want to underrate him,' said Phil. 'Us cockneys think we're the only smart ones on God's earth, but we're not. They just do things a bit slower down this neck of the woods, eh, Peter? The Super had to make doubly sure of your statements before he let you all go. We're all suspects, after all. Except, naturally, Mr Lillywaite. And Raicho.'

There was a moment's silence at this. They all looked at their plates and none of them looked at Raicho, who, sallow and handsome, was following his father's words closely. The fact was that nobody quite dared query the exemption of Mr Lillywaite from suspicion, but every one of them had a strong urge to query Raicho's. Finally it was Digby who did so.

'I don't really see that your son is out of it,' he said.

'After all, we've only his word for it that he came over when he did. In fact, he could very easily have been here that night.'

'Except that he wasn't,' said Phil. 'Because he came over when I telegraphed him the money.'

There was another silence as they thought this over.

'You telegraphed him?' said Dixie harshly. 'Why in hell did you do that?'

'*When*, precisely, was this?' asked Mr Lillywaite.

'As soon as I heard that Dad had been done in, and when the Governor told me I might be able to leave clink early. Sunday. I'd been thinking of Raicho, naturally, since our little conversation of the day before, Mr L.'

'But how—?'

'Borrowed the money from the Guv'nor,' said Phil cheerily. 'Silly old berk, as you'd probably agree, but useful at times. I think this is one loan I'm going to pay back. Raicho got it on Sunday evening, travelled on Monday, went to our old address, where he thought we'd be, then came on here.'

'I don't get it, Phil,' said Dixie.

'Don't you, Dixie? Let's just say, like I told the Super, it was a sort of insurance policy. For me, for Cliff—'

'Cliff?' said the Countess. 'What are you going on about, Phil?'

'Cliff, or Gareth, or whoever. Cliff, mother mine, is the oldest of the kids of Dixie's and my marriage that's actually legit. Technically. Mr Lillywaite and me established that when we went over things in jug. And I thought it might be as well if I advertised to all and sundry just who the next Earl of Ellesmere would be if I got my packet. I'd look after Raicho, I thought, and he'd look after me. And that's how it's turned out. That's why I've been parading him, telling the press he's the new Lord Portsea, and so on. Because even then, in Daintree, when I heard of Dad's death, it did seem to me that there'd been too many deaths of Spenders in the last few months.'

'You can say that again,' said the Countess.

'There was the old Earl—well, he *was* old, so that may very well have been above board. This young bloke, he sounds as if he was a bit of a tearaway, so perhaps no one was all that surprised when he tore away once too often and got his number on the M1 or wherever. Wasn't surprising *at the time*. But it did become a bit fishy-like when poor old Dad's number also came up a few weeks later. Who's got it in for the Spenders, you felt like asking?'

'I know nobody had it in for your dad *as* your dad,' said the Countess. 'He was one of the best.'

'I said he was the only one of us that was any good,' said Trevor, looking around.

'And you never said a truer, Trev,' agreed Phil. 'No, I just couldn't see Dad as having some deadly enemy he'd made over the counter at Blackwood's the ironmonger's. Nor any mortal foe in the saloon bar of the Prince Leopold in Clapham. The worst Dad ever behaved to anyone, by all accounts, was when he bawled out this 'ere butler and cook. And no one can say they didn't ask for it.'

'Personally my money's still on them,' said Digby.

'I might put a quid each way if they hadn't practically asked to be hauled in by going off to the new job with the loot still stashed away under the back seat of the car. If they did it, they were either mentally deficient, or they were playing a pretty funny game. Anyone for more veg?'

No one, it seemed, wanted more veg.

'Phil,' said the Countess, 'I think you know.'

'Me, Ma? I don't know much more than the rest of you. But I think there's one thing we've all been forgetting, as I told the Super yesterday. He's been following it up, since he heard.'

'What's that?' demanded Trevor.

'Three or four months ago—first time he'd done it—Dad made a will.'

'Well, we know that,' said Trevor. 'Don't rub it in. But it's irrelevant. It was cancelled out by the later one, so old—so Mr Lillywaite said. I'd have been rolling if the earlier one held.'

'So you would. Just one of life's little disappointments, Trevor, old mate. But what I wanted to know was, why all of a sudden did he make a will?'

They looked back at him, puzzled.

'Nearly fell under a number fifty-nine bus,' said the Countess. 'Even as it was he hit his head on the radiator. Got concussion. He was in the East London General Hospital for three days. Right as rain afterwards, though.'

'That's it. I didn't hear about it at the time, because I was in stir, and we're not really a writing family, are we? But it does seem to me that one or other of you might have thought of it. Because it was only five or six weeks later that he came into all this.'

They all sat over their pork, and only Trevor was munching away. Trevor had the sort of metabolism that impelled him to eat ravenously, yet always left him pencil slim.

'Worth thinking about, eh? That's what the Super thought, when we discussed it. Because what if whoever did it this time had in fact had a go before? And when that attempt failed, they were a bit unsure of things, and before they knew where they were, he'd come into the big money.'

'You've lost me, Phil,' said his mother bluntly. 'When he had that accident your dad didn't have no money. Only just in the black at the bank, and the tail end of the mortgage to pay off. What would be the point of pushing him under a bus?'

'Well, forget that for the moment, Ma, and let's think about Saturday night.' Phil looked around the table with the concern of the good host for his guests' welfare. 'Eat up, everyone. Nothing worse than cold Bisto gravy. Well, now: one of the things the Super and I are in total agreement about, is that someone took advantage of that pair who'd camped out in the attic (and serve 'em bloody right too). He planted stuff on them, some time during Saturday night. That lets out me, and Raicho, of course, and Mr Lillywaite. Oh, but wait a sec: Mr Lillywaite wasn't at the party, so you wouldn't think he could take advantage of this priceless pair, any more than I could. But what if this Parsloe phoned him after they'd been found out? What if Lillywaite had known they were there the whole time? What if Lillywaite had put them there as spies? Just possibilities, no more. So let's put Mr Lillywaite back in, very tentatively. No offence, old man.'

'I have no doubt the police will have considered me as a possible suspect, along with everybody else,' said Mr Lillywaite in a decidedly tight-lipped way.

'And I'm sure they rejected the idea as unthinkable,' said Phil. 'As we all do. Now, go back to Saturday night: the point of it is that it created two perfect scapegoats. If anyone—anyone in this house, anyone who knew of the discovery—had been thinking of murder, here were two sitting ducks to pin it on. The idea being that they were helping themselves to a modest share of the house's valuables prior to departure, were surprised in the act by Dad, panicked, and killed poor old Dad in the scuffle. That's what we were meant to think.'

'I still do,' said Lady Joan. 'They could have got over-confident.'

'Well, you just hug that thought to you, Joanie, which I must say shows great loyalty to the family, even if it is bloody feeble-minded. Now, if you wanted to give that impression, what would you do? First, load up their car with a few bits and pieces from the house. How does he (or she) know which car? Well, the estate hasn't got many cars, and this was far and away the oldest and shabbiest. It also had a London numberplate, while all the other numberplates were local. The only other car belonging here was the young Earl's sporty Jag, or whatever it was, and it's still in a garage being done over by the insurance people. *And*, now, by the police.'

'You know, I'm sure Dad said something about that car when he got back to the Drawing-Room that night,' said Trevor. 'Said the old Escort must have been what they were using.'

'Did he, now? Right, that's interesting. So, when everyone's gone to bed, and are snoring happily, our man—or woman—picks up a few things from here, pretty much at random, and takes them out to load up their car with. Probably nearly got caught doing it, too, because Parsloe and whatever-her-name-is came out to get a map from the car, so the Super tells me, and our person had to skip into the shadow of the old oak near the stables. All that precious pair notice, or think they notice, is perfume. And that doesn't tell us much, does it? Grown men slap it on these days.'

'Your son wears a hell of a lot of aftershave,' said Dixie.

'Quite. I slap a bit on myself, and so did Dad. And you can pick up make-up just from being with a woman, can't you? Provided you're close enough long enough. Anyway, this Parsloe and Nazeby (that's the name) go back in, and our chappie—lady, or whatever—gets back in the way he came out. No special housebreaking techniques needed. I expect he just hopped out of one of the windows, left it unlatched, then hopped back in.'

'What happened then?' asked the Countess, foreboding throbbing through her fruity contralto.

'Well—this is the nasty bit, Mum: Parsloe and Nazeby—what a combination of names, eh? Sounds like a

olicitor's firm. You should have taken them into
partnership, Mr L.: Lillywaite, Parsloe and Nazeby.'

'Lord Ellesmere, I really must protest—'

'Just a joke, old sport. The well-known and much-loved
ockney brand of humour. Well, this pair goes off to bed,
and they're as far away as they well could be from where
he action is going to be. Because the next thing for our
nan was to get Dad up. And he was in the State
Bedroom, just a short way down the Long Gallery from
he landing. Now Dad was a very light sleeper. Parsloe
and Nazeby found that out. We all knew it. Cat walks
along the guttering and Dad's out after it, heaving his
lippers at it. Because when he was disturbed—poor old
Dad—he did tend to go out and investigate.'

'We knew that,' said Trevor, 'but who else did? Are you
aying it was one of his own family?'

'Just doing a bit of narrowing down again, that's all.
Who else could have known? Not you, Mr Lillywaite, I
don't imagine. Nor you, Michele. Or have you been
leeping with Trevor at home recently? Chokey, now: he's
lept at ours often enough to know. Then there's Sam:
ould he have known?'

'It wasn't a matter of general comment in Haig Street,'
aid Sam, at his suavest, 'but I could have known.'

' 'Course you could. You could have picked it up in the
Prince Leopold, for example. So all that was necessary
vas a light noise—repeated if necessary—to get him up.
Now, the Super found something, didn't he, Sarge, that
night have a bearing there?'

'Could be,' said Sergeant Medway. 'He found some
arth in the little blind passage that leads off from the
anding. Dust had been disturbed on the floor there, and
n a big old brass jug that sat on one of the small tables.'

'Yes, that's what the Super told me. Now—'

'How come you're so friendly with the Super?'
emanded Trevor.

'He's decided my alibi is just about unbreakable,' said Phil, unperturbed. 'Quite apart from the fact that the fuzz always likes to keep in with the local gentry. Now what I think happened was this: that brass thing was banged against the wall a couple of times. Then the murderer—let's call him that—kept in the dark of that little passage until it actually worked, as it was bound to. Out comes Dad to investigate. And there it is (sorry Mum): karate chop to the neck as he stands peering down into the hall, and over the banisters with the body. Nasty, Ma, but quick as a flash. He would hardly have felt a thing.'

'It makes sense,' said Peter Medway. 'It definitely makes sense. But does it get things much further? Lots of people do a bit of amateur karate these days.'

'So they do. I took it up in jug. It's marvellous what you can pick up in there—real little further education centre the choker is, these days. Who else could have managed the blow? Trevor did a bit of karate before he took up with sex. Dixie did one of those courses—didn't you love?—to show women how to deal with rapists.'

'As if anyone would dare,' muttered the Countess.

'Chokey used to be a whizz at PT and stuff, though you wouldn't think it to see him now. Sam—I bet he's got a black belt or something. You nigs are always hot on those things, aren't you?'

'That's right. We nigs are,' said Sam, still very suave.

'So the karate chop doesn't narrow things down much. Who knows whether Digby didn't take a course in his lunch-break, in the intervals of whittling down insurance claims.'

'In point of fact I never did,' said Digby.

'We'll take your word for it, Dig. For the moment. Now the only question left is, who was it, and what was the motive? Was it someone who knew about the new will leaving the lion's share to me? Or was it someone who thought the old will was still in operation, splitting the loot up three ways? Or wasn't it anything to do with the wills at all?'

Phil beamed round at everybody.

'That's what the cops are going to have to decide, isn't it? Right: second helpings, anyone? Raicho, Sarge, go and get the rest of the pork and veg from the kitchen.'

The bustle of fetching fresh supplies did not lessen the tension around the table. Some of the guests busied themselves with finishing up their last scraps, or helping themselves (with no great relish) to more. But all of them kept their eyes on Phil, and all of them seemed convinced he had a lot more to say. Mr Lillywaite dissimulated most convincingly, as befitted a lawyer. He said 'A most interesting demonstration,' in a highly judicious manner to Digby, and nodded around the table.

'You know who it was, don't you, Phil?' said Joan, when they were all back at table.

'Me, Joanie? Like I said to Ma, I don't know any more than the rest of you. And I'm not a bleeding detective. We can leave the magnifying-glass stuff to the Sergeant here, and his boss. Of course, I have a few ideas . . .'

'Like what?' demanded Trevor.

'I don't know if he's said this to any of you, but one of the things the Super finds it hard to believe is that we didn't know we were next in line for all this boodle. But we didn't, did we? It wasn't something that ever occurred to us. We didn't even speculate about it. We sometimes said, for a laugh, that Dad was nephew to a belted Earl, but we never looked into it any closer. Did we?'

' 'Course we didn't,' said the Countess. 'We had better things to do with our time.'

'On the other hand, we could have. Joanie's the scholar: she might have looked it up. Digby's sharp—aren't you, Dig? Got to be sharp in the insurance business. Might be interesting to go round the various libraries and see who's been consulting the Peerage. But I must say I never thought about it. You didn't either, did you, Dixie? Trevor never pulled rank at the Labour Exchange — about the only thing he didn't pull, in fact. The rest of you — well, it's not even worth investigating Sam, I don't suppose, or Michele: you weren't even going with Trev till a few weeks ago, were you, love?'

'She could have started going with him *because* she found out,' said Joan, in her prim little voice.

'Kick my ego as you pass,' said Trevor.

'And then there's Mr Lillywaite. Of course, he knew. That was something he had to know, in the course of his duties. I bet he wished he'd taken it a bit more seriously when the young Earl died. And for all we know Parsloe could have known. You might think ahead a bit if you had a hard-drinking, hard-driving young master of twenty-three.'

'I bet it was often mentioned in the house,' said Digby.

'You could be right. As a remote, disastrous possibility. And there's another thing: I bet people talked about it in the village and round about. I've been in some of these country pubs around Daintree — sort of unofficial pass, you know — and the doings of the local nobs was very much chatted over there, over a glass of piss-poor local ale. Nothing much escaped the elders of the villages around Daintree, I can tell you. Got on my wick, rather when they could have been talking about football.'

'I don't see what that's got to do with it,' said Trevor 'Unless it was an outsider. And why would an outsider break in and do poor old Dad in?'

'That wasn't really what I was thinking of,' said Phil He became pensive, and began to toy with the food in front of him, and to look around the walls. 'Funny how you change in gaol. People say it never does anyone any good, and that may be true, but it certainly changes people. I expect you've noticed.'

'Yes, I have,' said the Countess. 'I thought at first you
were the same, but you're not.'

'No. Oh no. It's sort of . . . stiffened me. Given me a
purpose. Not like missionaries and that, but in another
way. 'Course, it taught me a lot of new lurks, as well. If I
hadn't come into this, I could have proved a right villain
when I got out. The tricks they teach you! We was right
amateurs, Chokey, old boy!'

Chokey grinned uneasily, and rolled his eyes sideways
at Peter Medway.

'I suppose we were, Phil.'

'Left our fingerprints on every job, speaking
metaphorical. I laughed, in Daintree, when I read the
local papers about that job at Brycenorton Towers.
Creased myself up, no kidding.'

'Brycenorton Towers?' asked Trevor, puzzled.

'Them classy neighbours I went a-visiting yesterday.
They was robbed last March. I read about it in jug, and
that's why I went over there—to hear about it. It had
all your fingermarks, Chokey, old pal.'

'Here, Phil—shut up: there's a cop here.'

'He's off duty, Chokey. Just here as a pal.'

'Anyway, I never had anything to do with that job.'

'Come off it, Chokey: I spotted you a mile off,' said
Phil, and his smile at his erstwhile partner was one that
Dixie herself might have envied for its ferocity. 'You was
in the local, right? Chatting up the servants from the
Manor on their night out. And your new partner was in
the house itself, doing the job. You do the research, and
the safe bits on the night, while the other bloke gets
landed if things go wrong. I'd have recognized you a mile
off, even if the description in the papers hadn't tallied.
Typical of you that you fucked the whole thing up.'

'I never did, Phil. I wasn't on that job.'

'Showed so much interest in the local gentry and their
houses that one of the locals got suspicious. Rang the

police. Shouldn't be too difficult, Chokey, to find out just
which of the local nob families you found so interesting.'

'Not difficult at all,' came the fruity country voice of
Superintendent Hickory. Appearing in the doorway, he
seemed to take over the whole space, like some sort of
road block. He gazed at Chokey like an agricultural show
judge who knows when the fine fruit and vegetables will
prove to be rotten inside. 'I've been talking to the
inspector who was on that case, and Mr Cartwright—'

'Chokey to his pals,' said Phil.

'Chokey Cartwright got them talking about the local
toffs, and they got round to the subject of the Spenders.
Mr Cartwright was so fascinated they never got off it, so
that when the police got the warning phone call, the first
place they came to was here. It was only when they'd
made sure that nothing was going on at Chetton that they
began to spread their net. They surprised a chap at
Brycenorton, but he got away through a back window. By
then, of course, Mr Cartwright had long ago evaporated
from the local.'

'See what I mean, Chokey? All your trademarks.
Especially the evaporation. A real little artist at getting
out from the under, that's you, Chokey. All these three
years rotting away in jug I swore you and me would do a
job where I was the one who got out from under, and you
was the one who got landed in it.'

'You can't mean it, Phil,' protested Chokey, his bleary
eyes taking on a pleading expression. 'You said you didn't
bear no grudge.'

'I did, didn't I? I practised that letter I wrote you five
times before I got it right. Right muggins I made myself
sound. I could hear you rubbing your hands, I really
could. It wasn't so very difficult, really, to get the right
tone, because a muggins is what I'd been all my life. But
what I didn't know then was that your little chat with the
local yokels in the snug bar of the Dowley Arms had given

you a bright idea, grand visions like you'd never had in all your years of petty crime.'

'Phil, I know what you're going to say, but I never—'

'And that idea was based on the information you got there that your pal Phil, best friend a man ever had, greatest mug and fall guy in the business, was only three steps away from a whacking great fortune. And if he came into it, you'd be on the gravy train for life: open-handed Phil would see you never wanted all your days. What he didn't give could be filched out of him. So you decided to help things forward a bit. Nice of you, Chokey. Thoughtful. I appreciate it.'

'I never knew nothing about the fortune. I was surprised when your dad came into it. Ask Dixie.'

'So you went to the library and checked the facts, I bet. Did you ask the nice lady at the desk to help you, Chokey? I bet you did: we're neither of us much of a hand with books, are we? Not wise, though. The nice lady might remember you. Sharp-eyed little librarian type, I wouldn't wonder. Then you decided to eliminate the two links in between. That's why Dad was worth pushing under a bus, Mum, even before he came into the fortune. So you came down here, didn't you, Chokey, and you fiddled with the young Earl's car. Crafty mechanic you've always been—dab hand with burglar alarms and suchlike. Then you went back up to London, got behind Dad on his way home from work, and gave him that hefty shove.'

'I never would've, Phil. We were mates, your dad and I.'

'And *I* know just what being a mate of yours means, Chokey. Anyway, you buggered it up, as per usual. Dad didn't die. What's more—nobody here knows this—a lady in the crowd went along to the Clapham police immediately afterwards and said she'd seen Dad pushed. They didn't take it seriously at the time. They did go

along and talk to Dad when he came round, but he pooh
poohed it, and said they mustn't say a word to Mum. Yo
know what police are like: male chauvinists to a man
They just said, "some hysterical woman", and laughed
off. But they've got her name and address, and she sai
she'd know the man again.'

'Poor old Perce,' said the Countess, dabbing her eye.
'If only he'd said.'

'That's it, you see: that was the trouble. Dad was a
innocent. So, first the old Earl pegs out—naturally
completely naturally, I imagine—and then the young
Earl goes off the road. And Chokey finds Dad in charge
and death duties hanging over the place, with more
pay— if I was to come into the fortune in the future
There ought to be a vote of thanks in the Commons
you, Chokey, for the sums you personally have manage
to siphon off into the Chancellor's pocket. So you cam
down here to see how the land lay, whether it was sti
worth it, whether Dad had made a will since he inheritec
how much I would be getting.'

'Everyone thought he was going to divide it up
protested Chokey. 'It wouldn't have been worth it.'

'It would still have been worth it,' returned Phil. 'Yo
realized that when you began to price the mountains
stuff here. Anyway, we can leave all that to the police
can't we? I don't think you'll be leaving here th
afternoon, Chokey. Not under your own steam, anyway
Right, everybody? Here endeth the first lesson. No puc
I'm afraid. I'm not much of a hand with apple turnovers

'If Mr Cartwright will just come along and answer a fe
questions,' came the rich, falling, cider-imbued tones c
Superintendent Hickory, advancing massively from th
doorway, while Peter Medway came capably up o
Chokey's other side.

It was a moment for some magnificent gesture—th
moment for Chokey to hurl defiance, to call for th

downfall of the ruling classes, to make a run for it and hurl himself over the balustrade, even if he only landed up in the fountain. But Chokey was not up to grand gestures. He looked shiftily from face to face, and for one moment Sam thought he might enunciate the ultimate in petty crooks' clichés: ' 'Ere, you're not going to pin this one on me.' But even that was beyond him. He started one sentence, started another: 'I never—', 'You can't–', and then the sentences petered out into whimpers, and Chokey let himself be led along out of the Dining-Room, and along the passage to the Pink Damask Room. Chokey had never been shaped in the heroic mould.

CHAPTER 16

THE COURTYARD

The party was over, that was clear. Phil sat, exhausted from his effort, gazing ahead blankly. The rest of them were pushing back their seats, whispering among themselves, reassuring each other that it was all over.

'Oh, *Phil*,' said the Countess. 'You were clever. I knew it was never one of the family did that to Perce. Now I can go home happy. You won't mind if I go home now, will you, Phil? All I want is to wipe the dust of this place off my shoes. Come on, Trevor.'

The Countess's instinct seemed to be shared by most of the rest of them. When Mr Lillywaite said, 'Most impressive,' they all echoed it, and some of them shook Phil by the hand, but they all began to make going-away noises, and soon they were all collecting up their luggage from the Hall. The little piles of cases and bags around Sir Philip's Staircase vanished one by one, as they all went out into the sun of the courtyard. Phil dragged himself out of his chair to follow them, to do the decent thing in the way of goodbyes, but he had somehow impressed them in such a way that none of them had much they cared to say to him.

Digby, it is true, did make one more attempt to get from him a statement on the subject closest to his heart.

'Er—you didn't say anything about your intentions, Phil,' he began, as Phil stood supervising the departures and making preliminary waves from the top of the stairs leading down to the courtyard.

'Didn't I, Digby? Well, on thinking it over I didn't think it necessary. That says it all.' Phil took Digby by the shoulders and swivelled him round, pointing up above the door. There, carved in stone relief, were the shield and motto of the Spenders. 'Ever heard the family motto, Digby? "*Je maintiens*". Which I interpret to mean "What I have I hold". And haven't we ever, over the years! Dad would never have made a true Spender, but I think I'll be following in their footsteps, at least in that respect. Goodbye, Digby. I expect you and Joan will do all right out of things, one way or another. You always have done. Give my regards to Wandsworth.'

And Phil smiled and waved and did his imitation of the general family favourite as one by one the cars pulled out of the courtyard and aimed themselves along the long road to the gates, and to the hordes of reporters still avid for photographs of any of the main actors in the Chetton drama.

Now there were few of them left. The children were playing with Sam on the newly cut lawn, and Raicho, who had been watching the departures in his contained way, soon went over to join them. Mr Lillywaite was lurking in the shadows of the Great Hall, waiting for his new master to be free. And there was Dixie.

Dixie had been standing, a little apart, in the sun of the courtyard. No one said affectionate farewells to her. She stood there, baring her teeth, in the puce blouse she had arrived in, waving her fleshy arms at the departing cars like overweight royalty farewelling loyal troops off to foreign fields. Now she turned to Phil, her fearsome, inviting smile seeming to mask some inner uncertainty.

'You were marvellous, Phil. You really were. I never seen you like that. You really were thrilling. You sent me.'

'Don't be obscene, Dixie. And don't try to have me on. You've always preferred your men weak.'

'Don't be rotten, Phil,' said his wife, with a nervous laugh. 'I'm willing to give the other sort a try for a change.'

'Oh no, Dixie. You won't get a chance. You just go and pack your bags and get off quietly, eh? We needn't go into the whys and wherefores. You just take the road, along with the rest.'

'Phil! What do you mean? I'm staying here with you!'

'No, you're not, Dixie. And it wouldn't be wise, would it, even if I let you. Because I left some bits out of my little reconstruction in there, didn't I?'

Dixie's face crimsoned with anger. She narrowed her eyes.

'What do you mean, left out?'

'Like how Chokey knew about the will that gave me the bulk of the boodle. Because he was right: the risk wouldn't have been worth taking if, after the Chancellor got his seventy per cent, the rest was cut into three. He knew that, for the moment, and if he acted fast, I was due to get it all. How did he know? Because you found out from Mr Lillywaite and passed it on.'

'Good heavens, Phil, I wasn't to know—'

'No? You weren't to know? Second point: Parsloe and Nazeby smelt perfume in their car when they went for the map that night. No, it wasn't bloody aftershave either— aftershave in the middle of the night? It was perfume. Here's one possibility: it had clung on to Chokey while he was in bed with you. You always did sling it on with a heavy hand.'

'Me and Chokey? It was me and Sam last. What do people think I am?'

'Most people have got a pretty good idea what you are, Dixie. I certainly have. These last three nights, while you've been freezing me out of the marital bed, I've been kipping down in Raicho's room. But since I came out of jug I haven't needed too much sleep. Got more than enough while I was inside, I suppose. So I've been alert to the toings and froings along the corridor. Chokey's been coming along to take my place, hasn't he, ever since the police guard was stepped down? Or was it just to talk things over?'

'Why shouldn't we talk things over? He's the oldest friend we've — I mean, he was the oldest friend we had.'

'Matter of fact, I've known about you and Chokey for months. Bloke who came to Daintree three months or more ago, he'd seen you out at the Bluebell Club — on our wedding anniversary. In fact, he'd seen you together all over the place.'

'Christ Almighty, Phil: I'm not a bleeding nun. I didn't know what Chokey was planning. You've never been jealous before.'

'No, I haven't. And I kept telling myself that you weren't to know what I was planning to do in the way of getting even with Chokey after I got out. But that perfume in the car — there's another possibility. Matter of fact, I don't think you and Chokey went to bed together that night. It would have been a bit odd, wouldn't it, if Chokey was planning to hop out and do Dad in. I think you hopped out of the house and stashed those things in the car. It was you that Parsloe and Nazeby thought they saw. And while you were out there coping with that side of the operation, Chokey was on the landing doing the indoor work.'

'Phil! You're joking! I never would!'

'I think you were in it, almost from the start, Dixie. Oh, Chokey got the idea, when he was down here on the Brycenorton job. But Chokey hasn't got the drive and the guts for a thing like this. You and he were in it together. And both of you had cast poor old Phil in the role of fall guy: he'd come into a fortune, and get robbed of it bit by bit by his wife and his wife's lover.'

'You got sick in gaol, Phil. You just sat there imagining things.'

'Of course, once you got down here, you changed your tack a bit, started fancying yourself as lady of the manor. But the basic idea was still the same: Phil is to come into his kingdom, and you and Chokey are to start raking in the shekels. Well, it just hasn't worked out, Dixie. Of course, as you've always known, I'm a generous soul at heart.'

'Generous? That's a bloody laugh.'

'Oh, but I am. I'm giving you a chance, Dixie. I could have said all this out over the table, couldn't I, but I didn't. Look, old Chokey's in there with the police now. There's a chance he won't split on you. Not, knowing Chokey, a very big one, but there you are. He was your choice. If he does split, there's a chance the cops won't believe him. They might well think he's just trying to pass the buck, which would be very much in character. And then there's the possibility that even if they do believe him, they won't do anything about it because they won't be able to get enough evidence to nail you in court. There: three chances. I'd say, as a betting man, that you've got a better than even chance of getting away with this.'

'Oh yes? And what's supposed to happen then? Me and the kids rot away for years on social security while you live in clover?'

'Oh no, Dixie, that isn't what I planned at all. As to

you, you'll manage, as you always have. Prosper, I dare
say. As to the kids, they stay here with me. And get this
straight: you try to get them, and I'll dob you in first
chance I get, and I'll go along with the cops till you're
behind bars, as you ought to be. They may not be all my
kids—'

'They're not.'

'—but they *feel* like mine. I doubt if they've ever felt
like yours, to you. They've never been anything but a
bloody encumbrance. So the kids stay here as long as I do.
And you go—you can have the house in Stepney for as
long as you need it. But you oppose the divorce; you
oppose my custody of the kids, and you're in for the
biggest trouble of your life. Got that, Dixie? Has the
message come through loud and clear? Right—we understand each other. Now hop it.'

Dixie stared at him in pink and puffy outrage.
Hovering on the brink of utterance was the bitterest
obscenity she could think of. She stared at him in silence
for half a minute, as if she was engaged in a final test of
wills. Then she straightened her shoulders, threw back
her head, and strutted into the house. Phil let out a great
sigh of relief, and strolled down to the courtyard. He was
still there ten minutes later, smoking a cigar, when Dixie
marched down the Great Staircase, through the Hall, and
out to her estate car. She threw the cases in, banged the
doors, and careered off down the road to the gates,
spraying gravel over the lawns where her children were
playing. Nobody waved her goodbye, and her own eyes
were set firmly ahead.

It was as he was watching the cloud of dust Dixie had
raised rising heavenwards that Phil heard from beside his
left elbow an apologetic cough.

'Oh dear, Lord Ellesmere, I'm afraid I heard all that. I
feel some deep misgivings about my part in this.'

'You, old cock?' said the Earl, turning to his man of

business. 'I don't know as you have anything to blame yourself for.'

'But if what you say is true I was clearly at fault in revealing (however cautiously and indirectly I may have put it) the contents of the late Earl's will to your wife.'

'You weren't to know the type she was, were you? It's taken me long enough to find out. I don't know what the ethics involved are, but I won't be making any move to get you crossed off the solicitors' roll, or whatever it is.'

'Do you think the police will get together a case against this . . . er . . . Chokey?'

'There's a pretty good chance. Chokey's not got much backbone. I'm betting on him breaking down.'

'And of course there's the woman who saw his attempt to kill your father earlier.'

'Yes, well — I'm hoping there won't be any need to call her. Because she doesn't exist. What you might call a figment of my imagination.'

'You made her up?'

'Don't look so bleeding shocked. The cops do it all the time.'

'Oh dear. At any rate, they can start with the robbery at Brycenorton Towers, and proceed from there. I hope, Lord Ellesmere, that we can have a long talk as soon as possible.'

'Natch. I've put aside the whole of tomorrow morning.'

'If you are going ahead with your plans to open this house as soon as possible — to the ghouls, as you call them —'

'Which I am. As soon as humanly possible. Sam there's writing a little guide. We'll have it duplicated in Meresham and sell it to them at some exorbitant whack. I'll be on hand all the first few weeks, with Raicho as relief. The kids will be around as long as the school holidays last. Noble family in residence — extra thrill if you can manage to shake one of the noble paws. We'll make a bomb, I can tell you. Then we'll start putting it on a proper footing.'

'It can't be too soon,' said Mr Lillywaite, with something of his old disapproval. He did not see Phil's look as he went on: 'You'll pardon me, Lord Ellesmere. I have the greatest sympathy for what you are trying to do, as you know. But is all this . . . blatancy necessary?'

'Of course it's necessary. If you don't pull in the crowds you don't pull in the money. It's only a superior sort of circus, this stately homes lark. If we tried to do it in the genteel tea-shop style you'd approve of, we'd be down the drain in five minutes.'

'I don't wish to sound . . . old-fashioned, Lord Ellesmere, but I see nothing wrong with a genteel manner of going about things. I have to confess that these last few weeks have been a great shock to my system. All that I held most dear has been assaulted—as if I'd been through a mental shock course. I am *not* squeamish, but I seem to have heard of nothing but (forgive me) petty criminals, illegitimate children, unknown heirs, pornographic films . . .'

He had gone too far. Phil planted his large hands on his hips and swung round to face him.

'Oh no. Just don't give me that. If we're going to work together in the future, you're going to have to snap out of that. I'm not going to have everything I do and say scrutinized and sniffed at with that kind of middle-class sneer. You can't tell me we're any different from the rest of the shower who've owned this pile. Oh, the old Earl sounded a decent enough old bugger, in a stiff-necked way. But our Trevor's never got up to much that the young Earl didn't get up to as well, I bet you. And what about the crew that went before? I read all about them in that book you left at Daintree. The founder screwed the county rigid, and so did the first Earl. There was the Countess who had it off with the groom, and the one who had it off with the interior decorator. There was the second Earl, who was a member of the Hell Fire Club—Trevor's a choirboy compared to him. And the fourth Earl who went to jug—am I supposed to feel inferior to him?'

'Every great family has it's skeletons.'

'Too bloody right. As I walk the corridors I can hear 'em dry bones rattling. That charming Victorian Earl who trailed Gladstone through the streets of London, hoping to catch him going into brothels. The one who shot his son—or was that the same one? The one whose wife arranged phoney séances for people who'd lost their sons in the First World War. The one who cleared half a million during the Marconi scandals. Don't tell me we're any different from them, mate, because I won't take it. We do the same sort of things. We just do them in a different accent, that's all.'

And the thirteenth Earl of Ellesmere nodded a curt farewell to his man of business and stomped across the lawns to join his children.

If you enjoy squirming
through scary books,
you'll shiver through the stories of

MARY HIGGINS CLARK

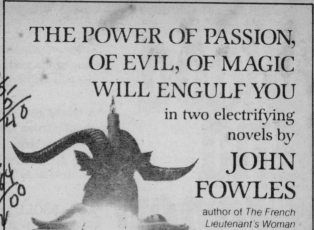